A Fine Summer Knight

JAN MARK

A Fine Summer Knight

Illustrated by Bob Harvey

VIKING

VIKING

Published by the Penguin Group
Penguin Books Ltd, 27 Wrights Lane, London W8 5TZ, England
Penguin Books USA Inc., 375 Hudson Street, New York, New York 10014, USA
Penguin Books Australia Ltd, Ringwood, Victoria, Australia
Penguin Books Canada Ltd, 10 Alcorn Avenue, Toronto, Ontario, Canada M4V 3B2
Penguin Books (NZ) Ltd, 182–190 Wairau Road, Auckland 10, New Zealand

Penguin Books Ltd, Registered Offices: Harmondsworth, Middlesex, England

First published 1995
1 3 5 7 9 10 8 6 4 2

Text copyright © Jan Mark, 1995
Illustrations copyright © Bob Harvey, 1995

The moral right of the author has been asserted

Filmset in Monophoto Baskerville

Printed in England by Clays Ltd, St Ives plc

A CIP catalogue record for this book is
available from the British Library

ISBN 0–670–85428–X

For Jonathan Appleton the Rippa Reader

Special thanks are due to the Brislands (Maidstone Branch),
Bilbo the Trader and Ulfstahm Herred of Norwich,
and Duke Henry Plantagenet.

Chapter One

'**A**untie, man, can we borrow your mirror?'

Salvo's head, with its knot of young dreadlocks like a nest of rampant garter snakes, slid round the door of Grace's bedroom.

'What's wrong with the one in the bathroom?'

'Bathroom's full of women,' Salvo said. 'Bathroom is heaving with the sisters and the grannies, and time's running out for Frank and Salvo.'

'All right, but don't make a mess,' Grace said severely, and backed away from the dressing table as Salvo shimmied into the room. On his heels came Grace's brother Frank. 'Anyway, what's the rush?'

I

'Elvis Look-alike Karaoke Night at the Fox and Hounds,' Frank said. He swept his long gingery hair into a rubber band on top of his head, at the same spot where Salvo kept the garter snakes, and let it fall around his face like a cascade of fibre-optics. Salvo, producing a small glass phial, applied a little rainbow glitter to his dreads.

'Elvis wasn't black,' Grace said.

'No, and he wasn't ginger either, man,' Salvo said.

'Neither of you look like Elvis.'

'Hell, no, Auntie. Nobody look like Elvis.' Salvo grinned at himself in the mirror and tried some glitter on his front teeth. 'That's the point.'

'Only time someone showed up who looked anything like Elvis he got booed off the stage,' Frank said. 'Spoiled it for everyone else. They gave the prize to Sally Cranfield, that night.'

'The point,' Salvo said, 'is *wanting* to look like Elvis. To feel the spirit of Elvis invade your every molecule.'

'Let's be frank,' said Frank, as he so often did, 'towards the end, even Elvis didn't look like Elvis.'

'Got any lipstick, man?'

'No, I haven't. I don't wear lipstick. Lipstick looks really cacky on someone my age,' Grace snapped, and slapped his hand away from the wicker basket of cosmetics. 'All that stuff's Helen's. What d'you want it for?'

'Eye shadow, man,' Salvo said. 'I am the vampire Elvis, this night. See me rolling red eye, me gleaming fang.'

Frank went into a spasm. 'It's-a-one, it's-a-two, it's-a-blue-suede-shoe.' His hip sent bottles rolling across the glass top of the dressing table.

'You clear that up before you go. I don't want to be here when Helen finds it.' Grace slipped between them and out of the door.

'Go, man, go!' she heard Salvo chanting. 'Hey, Frank, you think this glitter's poisonous?'

'Soon find out, man,' Frank said.

Which was worse, Grace wondered, going downstairs: being called man or being called Auntie? She was so much younger than the rest of the family that she had been an aunt before she was even born. Her eldest sister, Lynette, had brought her own son Paul to see the new baby.

'This is your Auntie Grace,' Lynette had said.

The name stuck. Grace went on being an aunt. People at school came in with news of little brothers and sisters; Grace just got nephews and nieces: Lynette's Paul and Joanne, Gavin's Louise, Jonathan and Josh, with another on the way. They were all too young to be any kind of company, except Paul, who considered himself too old. Her only hope was that there would not be any more for a while, after Gavin's latest. Alison, the next eldest of her sisters, lived in London. Frank and Helen were still at home with Grace. Helen had another year to go at school, and who on earth would marry Frank?

The Elvises came cantering down to the hall, paused for a last flirtation with the mirror beside the coat rack, and crashed out of the front door. The sisters and the grannies finished doing each other's hair and left the bathroom. Grace heard hairdryers start up in Mum's room and the one that she herself shared with Helen. She hoped Frank and Salvo had cleared up or she would be blamed for the mess on the dressing table. Helen was always accusing her of trying out her make-up and borrowing her clothes.

Gradually the house emptied. Helen went off to babysit for Gavin and Rachel's kids; Lynette and Mum headed for the Maid of Kent where they were bar-maids, Mum every evening and Lynette at weekends. Lynette always came over on Fridays for the weekly hairdressing sessions; it was almost the only time that Grace saw her. Dad had already left for a committee meeting and Grace, too old to need a babysitter and too young to be one, was left alone.

She did not mind; she was used to it. Helen, the next to her in age, had always been too old to play with her, too old even to have been at the same school. By the time Grace got to the Comprehensive next year, Helen would have moved on again. It seemed that she was doomed to arrive too late for everything, for she had been born one week past the limit for changing schools this year, dashing her hopes of joining Helen even for a few months, while she finished her A levels.

'Catch me ending up like Frank,' Helen had said. Frank was at the CFE, having his third go at GCSE Maths and Science, which was where he had met Claude Salvatore on day release. 'Rhymes with gory,' Frank said, when he first brought him home, but everyone called him Salvo

4

except for his girlfriend, Venetia, who insisted on Claude. Salvo was a plumber, but Venetia thought he could do better for himself. Salvo disagreed.

'How could I improve on me, man?' he demanded.

It was through Salvo that the Fordson had entered their lives. Salvo could empty a room once he got started on the intricacies of S-bends and union joints, but his real love, apart from Venetia, was vehicle restoration. The day that Frank first came home with his new friend, Salvo had stood transfixed in the doorway of the garage, gazing with love and wonder at the cattle-cake mill, the corn crusher and the stationary engine.

'Oh, this is heaven, man. Tell me it's true,' Salvo had cried. No one in the house had seen him yet, but they all heard his ecstatic yell.

'Frank's brought home a poet,' Dad said.

'Or a loony,' Helen said.

They were both right, Grace thought, but one man's loony was another man's poet.

Mum and Dad and Salvo took to each other right away. The cake mill had been Mum's gift to Dad on their twenty-third wedding anniversary, and the following year Dad had given Mum the stationary engine to run it with. By the time Dad had rebuilt the stationary engine another year had passed and they clubbed together to give each other the corn crusher. It ought to have been their silver wedding, but 'Every anniversary's an iron wedding with those two,' Lynette had said. Grace could scarcely remember a time when the garage, the drive and the back garden had not been crowded with machinery, metal-working tools and crates of parts, fly wheels and cog wheels and rusty iron relics that had been stripped for spares. Dad had just brought home a potato riddler on the back of Brian Milner's low-loader when Salvo appeared on the scene.

Salvo stood outside the garage and gazed at the stationary engine with a love-light shining in his eyes.

'Frank, Frank Thompson,' Salvo cried. 'You did not tell me, man, that you were a Thompson of that ilk.'

'What ilk, man?' Frank said, suspecting an insult.

'Steam-rally Thompsons!' Salvo roared.

Salvo, it turned out, never missed a steam rally. Throughout the summer he trekked around the county to places where steam rollers and traction engines congregated with every kind of lesser historic vehicle. Knowing that he could not hope to lay hands on a traction engine, he had bought an old Fordson coal truck in part exchange for his mountain bike, intending to restore it to its original condition. He then planned to attend rallies as an exhibitor, coming home with the brass commemorative plaques which Grace helped Dad to hand out every year at their own steam rally on Arling airfield. Salvo's coal lorry was kept on sufferance in the yard behind the block of flats where his family lived on the top floor.

'And the criminal element,' Salvo said, 'is reducing it daily. From 1947 to 1991 my Fordson lived and died with dignity. But those grave-robbers —'

he meant the criminal element '– are plundering it down to the axles.'

Somehow Salvo's Fordson found its way on to the back of Brian Milner's low-loader and shortly afterwards appeared in the Thompsons' drive, where it had stood for the last three years while Frank and Salvo spent every moment and every penny they could on restoring it. Dad was as usual organizing the Historic Commercial Vehicle class at the Arling rally this year, and Salvo had entered the Fordson.

'You joking?' Dad said, when Frank handed him Salvo's completed entry form. This had been nine months ago, when the lorry had been little more than a frame and looked like a vehicle that had been gutted by fire.

'We'll have it ready,' Frank had said. 'If we know you've got the entry form we'll be sort of challenged to get it finished.'

'Yes,' Dad said, gloomily. 'You'll wait till I've put it on the programme before you decide you can't get it done on time.'

'Salvo says we can get it done on time,' Frank persisted, refusing to take back the entry form.

'I suppose I'll have to give you the benefit of the doubt,' Dad said. People tended to take Salvo seriously. No one took Frank seriously. But it was beginning to seem as if Salvo might have been wrong, for once.

In Frank's bedroom lay a pile of loose-leaf folders, giving the whole history of the Fordson from the day it was first put on the road in 1947. After it

7

became Salvo's Fordson and not just MTW 641, the record was photographic.

'First principle of restoration,' Salvo said, 'photograph *everything*.' The earliest pictures showed a rusty wreck, with a worm-eaten float, which was the proper name for the wooden part at the back. Before the woodworm could get out and riot through the Thompsons' house, eating everything in its path, Salvo and Frank had taken away all the wood and burned it, after listing each part and photographing it. The cab had a wooden framework and that had to go too. When Grace looked at photographs of the Fordson at that stage she wondered how they had been able to bear to go on; there seemed to be almost nothing left, just the chassis and wheels, with the steering column rising eerily from the engine.

Then things began to look up. The chassis was stripped, brushed down and repainted. Frank and Salvo built a new float out of ash wood taken from a derelict removal van, attached to two oak beams that Salvo had wheedled out of a man who restored timber-framed barns. Salvo happened to be repairing his septic tank at the time. His work took him to outlying districts and remote farms where people always seemed to have useful things lying around in outbuildings – things that were useful to Salvo, that is. The cab had been reconstructed from a hardwood garden seat that someone no longer wanted, the cab's panels from steel shelving that, at about the same time, someone else no longer wanted.

'People are pathetically grateful to plumbers,'

Salvo said modestly, 'especially people who do not have mains drainage.' That was before he came home with his best windfall yet: two replacement seats which one of his clients just happened to have at the back of his garage, and which were as rare as phoenixes, according to Salvo. 'Fordsons were very common,' he explained, 'but they were work-horses, never maintained, driven into the ground. Nearly always the engine outlasted the lorry.' That was the biggest miracle of the lot. No matter what state the Fordson was in, the engine always started.

Sometimes, when Salvo was unable to busk his supplies out of customers, he and Frank would take off in search of replacement parts that they had heard about through the Historic Vehicle Restoration Society, or from a magazine advert. As the year drew on it looked as if Dad would have to eat his words. The last pictures in the Fordson files showed the lorry standing out in the road, complete with cab and float and radiator grille. It even possessed headlights, found lying around behind a dairy in Faversham, but it was not yet wearing them. The Fordson's headlights had to be mounted on its mudguards, and there were no mudguards.

In the Thompsons' garage, behind the cake mill, a tea chest housed the original mudguards, eaten away by rust and as lacy as cobwebs.

'Can't you patch them with resin?' Grace asked, hoping to sound knowledgeable.

'Get thee behind me, Auntie,' Salvo said, deeply shocked. 'This has got to be kosher, no fibre-glass, no Araldite. Would we have bothered with real oak beams for the float and environmentally-unfriendly-sawn-up-garden-seats for the cab if we'd've been satisfied with pine? Would we have hitched to Walsall for the gearbox if we could have faked it? No, man, we insist on the genuine thing, all over. This baby leaves here for *real*. In any case,' he added, tenderly stroking the mud-guard's gossamer contours, 'you might just as well try to darn a string vest.'

'We need a wheeling machine,' Frank told her. He had shown her a picture of a wheeling machine. It looked rather like a gigantic G-clamp, two metres high and standing on end, and between its rollers a man was thrusting a sheet of steel which, Grace could see, was well on its way to becoming a mudguard, the kind on a Lincoln Convertible. But it was a very old photograph.

'Don't they make wheeling machines any more?' Grace said.

'Not like that,' Frank said. 'Anyway, a new one would cost about three grand. These days vehicle bodies are made of pressed steel. The only people who use wheeling machines are types like us, doing restoration.'

The back of the garage was at that time lit-tered with bits of tortured sheet steel from which Frank and Salvo were trying to patch together new mudguards, as well as skirts and scuttles, the panels that fitted on either side of the radiator grille.

'Can't you just bend it?' Grace said. The mud-guard in the picture of the wheeling machine was extravagantly curved, but the Fordson's mud-guards looked quite simple.

'No!' Salvo howled. 'It doesn't just curve one way, it's three-dimensional.' He described three-dimensional curves with his hands, rather as he described Venetia. 'You bend it – you weaken it. The wheeling machine changes the molecular structure.' He saw that Grace was beginning to look blank. 'Like rolling out pastry,' he explained. 'You don't pull it, do you? You e-e-e-ase it.'

Dad took in a number of magazines: *Practical Classics*, *Old Glory*, *Vaporizing* for the stationary engines and *Steaming* for the traction engines, and Salvo searched them feverishly for people advertising wheeling machines. Grace studied the classified ads in the local free sheets, but although people were anxious to sell knitting machines, sewing machines, washing machines and rowing machines, in the two years that she had been looking no one had yet offered a wheeling machine for sale. Frank said that things were often discovered by word of mouth, but when she mentioned it at school no one knew what she was talking about, not even the teachers.

It was becoming a matter of some urgency now. The summer term had ended and in three weeks the steam rally would take over the old airfield at Arling. Salvo and Frank might have entered the Fordson in the Light Commercial Vehicle class, but it could not attend without mudguards and scuttles. Their honour was at stake.

In the hall the phone began to hoot: *Kadookah!*

Kadookah! The telephone always made Grace feel nervous when she was in the house by herself, partly because it was an illegal model, brought from America by Lynette's brother-in-law and shaped like a 1932 Lincoln Le Baron Convertible Roadster. Lynette had given it to Mum and Dad on one of their iron anniversaries and Grace was sure that somehow British Telecom would find out and turn up one day to arrest them all. Perhaps they had special detector vans, like for television-licence dodgers, one of which might even now be lurking at the bottom of Nettlefield Close, aerials twirling.

More likely, though, it was Venetia, making a spot-check on Salvo. Periodically Venetia drew up timetables for Salvo's improvement, and enrolled him in evening classes and home-study courses, none of them leaving time for Elvis or the Fordson. Venetia thought that the Fordson was a dirty waste of time, and seemed to hold much the same opinion of Frank. Salvo could handle it.

'We *is* studying, man,' he would purr into the telephone. 'Great drops of sweat plummet on to our Open College course books. Great drops of *blood*. Great balls of *fire*.' He could get carried away.

Grace never knew what to say to Venetia. If Salvo was out she could not pretend that he was in because Venetia would demand to speak to him. Venetia was a one-woman detector van. Perhaps if she approached the Lincoln Convertible very slowly it would stop hooting, but it went on and on, as if whoever was at the other end knew that there was someone in the house. Could it really be the BT hitmen, waiting until she answered the phone so that they could burst in and catch her with it in her hand?

She lifted the receiver which was the body of the Lincoln – the buttons were on the chassis – and spoke into the boot. ('The *trunk*, man,' Salvo would correct her – he could speak American.)

'Hullo?'

'Where *were* you, in the loo?' A familiar voice rasped down the line. It was Stephanie Milner from over the road, who had lately taken to calling herself Steffi. She managed to make it sound as if Grace had no business to be in the loo when Steffi wanted to speak to her.

'Didn't think it was for me,' Grace said, which was true. It was hard to believe it was for her anyway. Steffi never wanted to speak to Grace.

'I've been waiting till everyone went out,' Steffi said. 'I've been watching. Is your dad home this evening?'

'Not till late.' What was Steffi up to? In the time it had taken her to dial the number and wait for Grace to answer she could have crossed the road and back.

'Right,' said Steffi. 'You've got a telescope, haven't you? I want to borrow it.'

'Yes – what for – no –' Grace said. The telescope was Dad's; before that it had been Grandpa's, his dad's, and it was a real one, powerful, not a toy. You could see the moons of Jupiter through it, or you could if you went right out into the country where there were no street lights.

Eventually the telescope would be Gavin's and once, years ago, he had taken Grace out on to the downs to watch an eclipse of the moon – just her, as a special treat. Apart from Dad, Gavin was the only one allowed to handle the telescope. It lived in a special leather case on top of the wardrobe in her parents' bedroom and even Frank kept his mitts off it. How had Steffi known about it?

'Well, you have, haven't you?' Steffi was saying.

'Yes, but I can't get it,' Grace said. She could feel her toes digging into the carpet, through her shoes. Not even Steffi was going to nag her into this. 'What do you want it for?'

'None of your business,' Steffi snapped automatically, because that was what she always said when Grace asked her questions.

'Yes it is,' Grace said, sure of that at least. 'Dad'll go mad if I touch it.'

'Well, he won't know, will he? Look, I need it while it's still light. Hurry up.'

'It'll be light till nine o'clock.'

'It'll *be* nine o'clock if you don't leave off arguing. Just bring it over. No one'll find out.'

'Is that why you rang, in case someone was still here?' She could imagine Steffi, ready to hang up if the wrong person had answered, like someone in a spy movie. 'Anyway, why do you want it?'

'I want to look out of the loft.'

'Is it finished?' The Milners, who owned their house, had been having an extra room built into the roof so that they could take in lodgers. For three weeks the house had stood corseted in scaffolding poles.

14

'No, but the stairs are in. I want to go up there now. There's something I want to look at,' she admitted reluctantly.

Carrying the Lincoln to the fullest extent of its cord, Grace moved to look out of the window by the front door. She could see the Milners' house opposite, with the scaffolding round it, and between the scaffolding, the new skylight in the Milners' roof, slightly open and reflecting clouds.

'You'll just be able to see our roof,' Grace said.

'I don't mean at the front. I want to look out the back. There's a *view*.'

'Why d'you need a telescope? Can't you just look at the view?'

'You can see better with a telescope, can't you?' Steffi seemed to realize that she was actually holding a conversation with Grace. She had almost begun to sound friendly but she put that right immediately. 'Just fetch it over, OK?'

'I can't, I told you. I'm not allowed –'

'No one will know. It's only for a few minutes, just till Mum gets back.' Wendy Milner also worked at the Maid of Kent. Her shift ended when Mum came on behind the bar so Grace knew exactly when she would be home. If she could keep Steffi talking long enough it might be too late to take the telescope over.

'I'm not supposed to go up there yet. The plaster's wet and the floor isn't finished,' Steffi went on. 'It's going to be my room, but I can't wait. There's something I specially want to look at *now*.'

'What if my dad finds out?' Grace said. 'Suppose you break it or something?'

'I'll let you come over and look too,' Steffi said. 'Oh, go *on*,' and then, incredibly, '*please?*'

Grace, prepared for hard bargaining, had been about to suggest this herself. There was no way she would leave Steffi alone with the telescope. She might not bother to bring it back in time, or in one piece. But if she too were disobeying orders, working against the clock, it might almost be worth risking.

'Just for a few moments,' they both said at the same time, Grace yielding, Steffi pleading. It was unheard of, Steffi doing anything other than issuing commands and put-downs.

'OK, then,' Steffi said, as if it were she who had made up her mind. 'I'll come out the front and keep watch. If I see anyone coming I'll wave you back in.'

'Just like that,' Grace mouthed into the receiver, as Steffi hung up. Steffi wouldn't get into serious trouble if her parents caught her in the loft conversion when she ought not to be there. The telescope really was serious; to be caught with it would mean serious trouble. It was valuable and unlike, say, the corn crusher, easy to break. But she thought of Steffi's pleading voice, Steffi saying 'please?'. Could this, at last, be her chance to make friends with Steffi?

Chapter Two

When she had first heard about the loft conversion Grace had pictured a snug dormer with its own little gable or, better still, something like a bungalow she had seen from the coach to London, where the tiled roof curved over two attic windows so that the building seemed to have eyebrows. She had imagined looking out of the front garden to see the Milners' house frowning down at her just as Steffi Milner frowned down at her, but after all nothing showed at the front except for that flat slanting skylight.

The Milners had lived across the road for as

long as Grace could remember. Grace had always hoped that she and Steffi could be friends, but Steffi was two years older and, having had the foresight to be born in August, three years ahead of her at school. When she was little Grace had had the vague idea that one day they would be the same age, that Grace would go on growing while Steffi somehow remained exactly the same, waiting for her to catch up. But the reverse seemed to have happened. Not only had Steffi continued to be older and bigger, she was also growing up much faster, already at the Comprehensive while Grace still had another year to go at Wing Farm Primary; Steffi past the 150cm mark while Grace had been humiliatingly stuck at 132 since Easter; Steffi's feet in 6s while Grace was still in 2s, hardly out of baby sizes.

Grace would not have known about these discouraging statistics but Steffi was Wendy and Brian's only child, and Wendy talked about her a lot, boasted almost. Coming as the last of six, Grace did not flatter herself that Mum any longer thought children were something to boast about. Probably she had got over boasting with Gavin, or at least with Alison.

Although the house was empty Grace went upstairs on guilty tiptoe as if afraid of leaving incriminating footprints. In her parents' room she took one precautionary glance out of the window to make sure that Steffi really was keeping watch from among the scaffolding poles, then stood on the end of the bed to reach the top of the wardrobe where the telescope lay in its leather case. A spiny, leggy thing lying alongside it was its tripod, but Grace did not suppose that Steffi was expecting her to bring that too.

She unbuttoned the case at one end, slid the telescope out and fastened the case again so that if the worst happened and Dad came home early, he would see nothing amiss. She had already put on her winter jacket with the thick padded sleeves. It would look odd on such a warm evening but the padding was just what she needed for concealment. She slid the telescope up the sleeve alongside her left arm and let the end rest in her cupped hand. It seemed to her a very professional thing to have thought of, almost worthy of a burglar. She left, burglariously, through the back door.

The Milners' front garden was stacked with tiles, piles of broken plaster, and sections of sawn-out beam and rafter from the roof. As Grace came through the side gate Steffi bobbed out from among the scaffolding poles and beckoned violently, but Grace, trusting her not at all, looked carefully down the Close before she crossed over. She did not need to look to the right. Theirs were the last houses, on either side.

'Well, where is it?' Steffi demanded in her usual voice, forgetting to sound friendly now that she was getting what she wanted. Grace lifted her left arm stiffly, and waggled her fingers over the lens cap. 'Come on in, then.'

Grace followed her round the tiles, under the scaffolding, to the back door. It was a long while since she had been inside the Milners' house, a long while since the days when she had gone over with Mum; and Mum and Wendy had pretended that little Auntie and little Stephanie were playing nicely together. That had been before the Milners bought their council house and started putting in new doors and windows and the loft extension. Inside, the house was just like her own, only the other way round and much tidier, with shiny woodwork . . . too shiny –

'Mind the paint!' Steffi barked, as Grace's rigid left arm went out of control in the doorway. She clutched it to her side like someone who had been shot in the shoulder, as they went upstairs.

At the end of the landing, where the Thompsons had a cupboard, a new flight of stairs ascended.

'Take your shoes off,' Steffi said. 'We don't want to leave marks on the wood. And don't touch that plaster.'

Grace had thought that the wall was painted a dirty pink and was wondering why the Milners had chosen such a dreary colour, but that was the plaster. She had expected it to be white and chalky, like when you broke your leg. She clutched her arm more firmly still and kicked off her shoes to follow Steffi, trying to pause at the skylight to see what her own house looked like from above, but Steffi hauled her on through the door at the top of the stairs and into a low, tent-shaped room. At one end was a window, and through the window was the view, but between Grace and the view another girl was standing, Sarah Carr, one of Steffi's friends from school.

'Got it, then?' she said, ignoring Grace. Steffi,

also ignoring Grace, took Grace's sleeve and eased the telescope out of it.

'Not very big, is it?' Sarah said disdainfully.

'It's quite powerful,' Steffi said, dropping Grace's sleeve and Grace's arm with it. Grace felt as if the telescope had put on her coat and crossed the road by itself, leaving her out of it altogether.

'How do you know?' she said and then, when no one answered, 'How do you know it's powerful?'

'Frank told me,' Steffi said. This had a strange effect on Sarah. She started to give at the knees and moaned, 'Swoon, swoon.'

'You feeling all right?' Grace said daringly. Sarah looked at the place where Grace was standing as if Grace were not standing in it. Grace began to wish more than ever that she was not; that she was back over the road and the telescope was where it belonged, in its leather case on top of the wardrobe.

Steffi, meanwhile, had opened the smeary window and was examining the view through the telescope. A wind was getting up, whining round the dormer and making the window vibrate on its stay. Steffi found it hard to hold the telescope steady and swore loudly.

'What are you looking for?' Grace said. It was clear that Steffi wasn't just looking at the view, she was searching for something. Steffi did not even bother to say 'None of your business'. She was leaning right out of the window now, as if getting one metre closer to the view was going to make any difference to a telescope that could see

21

the moons of Jupiter. Sarah opened the other window and gave directions.

'It's that street with the big white house at one end and a sort of garage place at the other ... past the bus depot ... now, halfway along, where the road goes uphill ...'

Grace, peering round Steffi's shoulder, examined the view without the benefit of the telescope. It was a disappointment. From Steffi's bedroom window, one floor below, she had seen it before, the hillside that lay across the Sittingbourne Road. It was not a very steep hill and from ground level it was hidden by houses and trees. Grace had supposed that in the loft, so much higher up, they would be able to see over the top of the hill, to the edge of the town, the fields beyond, maybe even to the river, snaking away between willows and under bridges. But the skyline looked exactly the same as it had always done and was exactly where it had always been. The only difference was that from up here they could see what lay behind the trees and houses on the far side of the allotments: the gable end of the bus depot with its red and gold sign, the upstairs windows of the printing works. And what before had looked like a jumble of roofs had become streets of houses, branching off the Sittingbourne Road and marching up the hillside in orderly rows before wheeling smartly and disappearing over the top. With the wind now sweeping cloud shadows across the landscape, the houses really did seem to be moving.

'Got it!' Steffi said triumphantly and settled down with her elbows on the sill. 'What's the time?'

'Ten past seven,' Sarah said.

'We've got ten minutes before Mum gets back,' Steffi snarled. 'Come on. Come *on*.'

'Can you see anything?' Grace asked nervously. She did not want to be here with the telescope when Wendy Milner got in; Mum might get to hear of it.

'Not yet. Don't jog me!'

Grace had come in too close. She retreated a pace or two and located what Steffi must be looking at: the corner halfway along that street with the big white house at one end and a garage at the other. She tried to work out what Steffi was searching for. The street was just a street, the houses just houses. Far more interesting were the patches of green, fringed with trees, that lay farther across the hill to the left of the streets, some kind of park or enormous garden, flickering in and out of focus as the cloud shadows passed over.

'There he is!' Steffi shouted.

'Is he on his own?'

'Ye-e-e-s. Told you. Fisher was lying, he's not going with anyone. He's wheeling his bike round the back – you can see right up the garden – he's going in at the side door. Oh, I wonder if that's his bedroom at the front. If the light was on you could see right in, swoon, swoon.'

It all became disgustingly clear to Grace. Steffi wanted the telescope to snoop on a boy she fancied. The disgust gave way to alarm. Suppose Steffi wanted to go on borrowing the telescope, kept nagging and threatening . . .

'Now he's coming out again – he's – he's – he's – oh!'

'What's up?' Sarah said.

'Lost him. He's gone off down the road.'

'On his own?'

'Think so.'

'At least you know where to look now,' Sarah said. Grace noticed that she was marking something on a map. It seemed incredible. The two of them had worked out exactly where this boy lived so that Steffi could sit at the window in her new room and drool over the house, watching for him to go in and out, swoon-swooning every time he appeared. Grace recalled Sarah going 'Swoon, swoon' when Frank's name was mentioned. What a horrible thought. She could picture Steffi keeping her vigil at the back for the unknown boy while Sarah lurked behind the skylight at the front and lay in wait for Frank. Frank! She ought to try living with him for a bit and then see how swoony she felt.

Steffi lowered the telescope at last and eased herself back into the room.

'Can I have a look now?' Grace said.

'What at?' Steffi said suspiciously, as if Grace might have designs on her fellow.

'I just wanted to look through the telescope,' Grace said, 'before I take it back. You did say –'

'Well, be quick,' Steffi said. 'And stay off of that plaster.'

Grace took the telescope, leaned her elbows on the window sill and trained the lens on the hillside. She had only seen the Universe through it before; she had not even begun to wonder what something much closer might look like. And, of course, everything seemed much closer still, but strangely flat, like looking at a photograph or as if the view were painted on a wall. There was the bus depot, as close as the end of the garden; she could see buses, people even; there was the white house. Grace searched for the green lawns and trees; she moved the telescope too far, swivelled it back and caught a panning glimpse of a long flat building near the top of the hill, a traffic light just turning from green to amber, two pointed poplars and a snatch of railings, a hedge. She steadied the telescope and settled on rows of pale figures standing beneath trees. What could they be? Some kind of a parade?

The sun went in and came out again fleetingly, and as the clouds slid away from a lawn among bushes, a person walked out across the grass, a person who shone. The sun struck him and he exploded into light as if he were made of burnished metal. A metal man? A robot? Grace blinked away the dazzle. No, not a robot, a knight; a knight in armour, with a helmet on his head and a sword in his hand, advancing towards the white waiting figures under the trees. Before she could believe what she had seen the clouds closed over, the shining vision had vanished, and Steffi's hand knocked the telescope out of alignment.

'Come on, that's enough. We don't want to get caught up here.'

Too surprised to protest, Grace let Steffi push her away and close the windows. Whatever she had seen was lost out there beyond the dusty panes amid the confusion of buildings and trees on the hillside, now tiny and distant again. When it first appeared she had almost cried out to Steffi, 'Look!' and Steffi would have grabbed the telescope to see for herself. And if she had, Grace would never have known what it really was that had walked on the hillside for that astonishing moment. But what was it – really? How could it be real? She could not have seen it; could *not* have.

'Go on, you'd better put it back.' Steffi seized the telescope and began to ram it down Grace's sleeve. 'I'll tell you if I want it again.'

'I can't –' Grace began, but Steffi manoeuvred her out of the door and down both flights of stairs, pausing only just long enough for Grace to scuffle into her shoes, and through the kitchen.

'Hurry up, hurry *up*.' Grace found herself stumbling among the rubble outside the back door. Her arm hit a scaffolding pole and the telescope clanged against it. The Milners' gate slammed behind her and she was left to race across the road and in at her own gate, with the telescope cold against her arm, pressing guiltily into her hand.

She scrambled upstairs and shoved it into its case on top of the wardrobe. It was not until she was back downstairs, in the kitchen, that she had time to think: I've seen a ghost. *I've seen a ghost through a telescope.*

And then, How can I see it again?

Helen woke her at one o'clock when she came back from Gavin's, and after that Grace could not sleep again. Long after Helen had dropped off she lay on her back, open-eyed, awake, alert, aware. Everyone was home now and in bed, except for

Frank, of course, who might not bother to come home at all. The house was still – or was it? The people in it were still, but the house itself made noises all the time: discreet clicks and sighs as the pipes and woodwork settled down; the occasional plops and trickles from the tanks in the roof. How much louder they would sound to Steffi, up there in her loft with them.

Grace was not afraid of the dark. She had been when she was small, but not any more. When she talked about ghosts Mum had said, 'Look, Auntie, Alison's in that bed and Helen's up above you.' They had had bunks in those days. 'Me and Dad are next door and Frank's on the other side. No one can get at you.'

'Ghosts can,' Grace had insisted, knowing that ghosts could move through walls. On one of the few occasions Steffi had bothered to speak to her she had informed Grace that after nightfall rotting corpses promenaded up and down the Close and sometimes seeped into people's houses, lay around under their beds . . .

'There are no ghosts in this house,' Mum said firmly.

'How do you know?' Grace put one fearful ear outside the quilt in order to hear her.

'Because no one's ever died in it.'

'How do you *know*?'

'Because we're the only people who've ever lived in it. I think I'd have noticed somebody dying.'

For a long while afterwards she had stopped thinking about what Steffi had told her until she found out that the house, the whole estate, had been built on farmland.

'Suppose somebody died in a field hundreds of years ago and that place where they died was where this house is?'

'Then the ghost will be down on the ground, won't it?' Mum had said. 'It won't be flapping around in your bedroom.'

'Suppose they died in a *tree*?'

'I've never heard of anyone climbing a tree to die.'

And now she *had* seen a ghost, not in the house, it was true, and not in the dark, but she had seen it, so clearly that she had almost convinced herself that she had heard it too, the clank of its armour, the rasping swish as it drew its sword. Or was she imagining that? Common sense told her, yes. Yes, you are imagining it. Whoever heard of seeing a ghost through a telescope? But she knew that whatever was imaginary had started back there in Steffi's loft; it was not something she had invented since. All right, the figure had not drawn its sword, it had not carried a shield, there was no plume fluttering in its helmet, perhaps it had not even been a knight, but it *had* been a man in armour. In that brief, flickering moment, as the cloud shadows and sunlight raced across the hillside, he had been there, walking towards the white waiting people across that patch of grass that might be a garden, might be a park.

But where was it, and how was she to find it? How was she to find her knight again? The obvious answer was to walk out of the house next morning, down the Close, turn right into Wing Farm Drive, cross the Sittingbourne Road and climb the hill to the place where two poplars grew by a row of railings, near a traffic light. It might be obvious, but it was not possible.

Too tired to sleep, Grace lumped over in bed and thought about it. She had worked out only recently that after Helen was born Mum had probably assumed that she would have no more children, so when Grace appeared six years later everyone, although pleased, had been taken by surprise. Mum had had to borrow back the baby clothes, the cot, the cradle and the buggy that she had given to Lynette. She had thrown up her new job and Helen had realized that she would not, after all, be getting the bedroom to herself when Alison left home. But somehow they had made room for Grace. The only trouble was, Grace thought, they had all got hopelessly out of practice and as far as she could see, they had never got into it again. Lynette and Gavin were gone, married, with their own families; Alison was long gone too. Frank had college to think about, and the Fordson; Helen had school and a Saturday job and belonged to a drama club. Mum was working again at the Maid of Kent, and three mornings a week at the launderette. Dad had just retired from the Post Office and was occupied by the steam rally and his restoration work. The household was no longer geared to children. Dad was as old as some people's grandfathers; he *was* a grandfather, Mum was a granny. They had been grandparents before she was even born, already an aunt.

The worst of it, though, was that everyone seemed to think that Grace must be permanently at risk, and that unless her every movement was monitored she might come to some harm. When she was little the cry had been 'Don't go out of the garden'. As she grew older and more adventurous it was 'Don't go beyond the end of the Close'. Now it had become 'Don't go off the estate', and except for visits to Lynette and Gavin, or trips to London, or tagging along with Mum and Dad to steam rallies, she never did get off the estate. She went to school on the estate, went shopping on the estate, played on the estate. All her friends, except for Lucy Claggett, lived on the estate and Lucy was only a hundred metres in the other direction, down Wing Farm Drive.

Then, last summer, the joy-riding started at night, and she had to be in early. Discarded hypodermic needles were found in the rec, so now that was out of bounds. Strangers in a car had been seen talking to children near the school, and she had to come straight home. There were no more trips to the bottle bank even, because that was where the glue-sniffers hung out. She could not put a toenail outside the gate without someone demanding to know where she was going and when she would be home, and the cry had changed to 'Don't go anywhere on your own!' But there was never anyone ready to go with her.

If Frank or Helen wanted to go exploring on the hillside beyond Sittingbourne Road they could do it without asking anyone's permission, and God alone knew where Frank got to sometimes, but they didn't want to. And they wouldn't want to go with her. She had thought that the world would grow bigger as she grew older; instead it was shrinking daily.

'*When* can I go places on my own?' she demanded.

'When you're old enough to look after yourself.'

She would never be old enough.

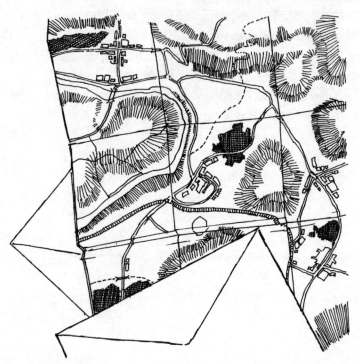

Chapter Three

'**I**f there was any justice in this world your dad would deliver his own mail,' said the postman.

'It's not all for him. Anyway, he's retired,' Grace said, as the postman filled her arms with packets and wads of envelopes, held together with wide elastic bands.

'Like I said, no justice. Know why we have a second delivery round here? Because your lot fills up the bag first time round.' He stumped down the steps. 'Not to worry, Auntie. Only kidding.'

'I know,' Grace said glumly. The postman must be a friend of Dad's or he would not have called her Auntie. She went inside and kicked the door shut behind her.

'Do you have to make that row?' said Frank, bleary in the kitchen. 'Think of my head, man.'

'Have you been drinking?' Grace dumped the mail on the table.

'Of course I've been drinking. We went to the pub, didn't we?'

'Then it's no good blaming me if you've got a headache.'

'I didn't say I had a hangover. Can't afford to get a hangover,' Frank complained. 'I just got a headache. Anything for me?'

'Rubber bands.' Grace skinned them off the bundles and handed them to him. 'That's probably why you've got a headache,' she added, looking at Frank's haggard face. 'Pulling your hair up tight like that. Have you been to bed?'

'Not yet.'

'Well, you've had that ponytail for *thirteen* hours. No wonder your head aches.'

'Oh, don't nag, Auntie,' Frank moaned.

'Who won the Elvis look-alike?'

'Oh, some New-Age fatso come in off the street.' Frank eased off the rubber band from his hair and hung it on his thumb along with the ones that Grace had given him. The hair hung dead straight below his shoulders except for a strange kink all the way round, where the elastic had cinched it.

'You look like something that crawled out of a crypt,' Helen said cruelly, wandering into the kitchen with a coffee mug. She pounced on the mail-strewn table. 'Anything for me?'

'I've sorted yours,' Grace said, handing her a couple of envelopes.

'It's no good trying to lick round me,' Helen growled, snatching them from her. 'Not after what you did to my lipstick.'

'I never,' Grace said, looking hard at Frank. 'I wouldn't touch your manky old make-up. That's the way skin diseases get spread.'

'It was Salvo,' Frank admitted sheepishly.

'Salvo wore my lipstick?'

'Not on his lips,' Frank said. 'He wanted it for eyeshadow.'

'That is the most disgusting thing I ever heard in my life,' Helen said, 'Nicking somebody else's lipstick for eyeshadow. You make me sick, both of you. Well, he can just get me another one. It's Plum Shimmer, by Rimmel.'

Grace went on sorting the mail while they argued over her head. None of it was for her, which was not surprising. The only time she got any post was when someone on holiday sent her a card. The packages were from Mum's mail-order catalogue; nearly all the letters were for Dad. Grace gathered them up and took them into the end of the living room that was his office. Two-thirds of the room really was for living in, with a three-piece suite and the television set, coffee table, music centre, bookcases. The office end had a filing cabinet squeezed in, and a desk. The bookcase there housed only books and bound magazines about vehicle restoration, industrial archaeology and steam traction; and rows of box files. In the no-man's-land where the one-third

34

met the two-thirds was the dining table. On the rare occasions that they all ate together they sat at the living-room end, or crammed round the one in the kitchen. The office side was occupied by neat stacks of stationery, small orange fliers for the Arling Valley Steam and Transport Bonanza. In the space between them Grace laid out the letters addressed to Mr Ron Thompson or to Hon. Sec. Arling Valley Steam Rally, who were one and the same person. Hon. Sec. meant Honorary Secretary. Grace had once thought that this must be a distinguished title, like for a lord or an MP, until Dad explained, 'You're thinking of Honourable. Honorary just means I don't get paid.'

'But that's not fair,' Grace had protested.

'Of course it's fair. None of us get paid. We do it because we like it.'

Several of the letters were late entries for the classes that Mum and Dad were stewarding: Stationary Engines and Historic Commercial Vehicles. Entries were supposed to have been in by the beginning of July, for the programme, but people went on applying until the very last minute, sometimes turning up without having applied at all. There was a note from the man who was bringing his Mortier fairground organ, another from the firm who were supplying the commemorative plaques, some bills and a receipt on the payment for coal for the traction engines. Grace did not read any of the letters but put them in separate piles to save Dad time later. Even on a Saturday he was out early, this time delivering the big Dayglo posters that would be put up in shops and on

35

hoardings. Nearer to the date of the rally Frank and Salvo would go out and staple the orange fliers to telephone poles and fences, for the council to remove immediately afterwards.

Dad was also in charge of arena events: the displays of majorettes and Morris dancers, cadet bands, sheep-dog shows, a tug-of-war between humans and a traction engine. Last year there had been can-can dancers on the back of Brian Milner's low-loader that trundled slowly round the arena. But there would also be a big display on each of the two days of the rally, something really spectacular: a helicopter rescue or parachute descents. This year it was to be a motorcycle stunt team. There was a letter from them too. Grace did not even open that one; the team's name, *Motomaniax*, was printed on the envelope, and the word URGENT was scrawled in red beside it. She looked around for somewhere to put it where Dad would see it first.

She liked to be able to help him. Since the bottle-bank embargo it was about the only interesting thing that she was allowed to do, and she took a diplomatic interest in the rally because it was family. If the weather was good the rally could be two glorious days of noise and steam, big wheels and heavy vehicles, fairground music, auto-jumble stalls and sideshows, ice cream, burgers and beer. It would be more glorious still were she not constantly reminded not to wander off, not to go with anyone, to stay out of the arena, to keep away from the camping sites, to steer clear of the machinery – all the things that only an idiot would not take for granted. She enjoyed the arena events, and if the Fordson ever made it to Arling airfield she would root for that as it went round in procession, with Salvo at the wheel and Frank on the float, but her real love was the traction engines.

The historic buses and cars and trucks might be old, but they were still recognizably buses and cars and trucks. There was no such thing on the roads as a traction engine nowadays. When they took to the field, shining, solemn and slow, it was like a pageant of people who had suddenly appeared from the past wearing clothes new and bright that you saw only dull and faded in museums. It was like seeing Queen Elizabeth I in her amazing farthingale, or Julius Caesar, or a knight in armour.

Grace paused, the *Motomaniax* letter in her hand. A knight in armour . . .

She went back into the kitchen where Frank and Helen were still snarling at each other.

She said, 'Is there a castle round here?'

'A castle?' Helen said. 'There's Leeds Castle. You know that, you've been there.'

'I know about Leeds,' Grace said. 'I meant *near* here, like . . . like up on the hill.'

'What hill?'

She pointed. 'Over Sittingbourne Road.'

'A *castle*?'

'Ruins. Well, somewhere with grounds. Or just a park. Grass . . .'

. . . a place where even by daylight a man in armour could step out in sunshine between one

37

cloud and the next; where still white figures waited among trees . . .

'What are you on about, grass or castles?' Helen was asking impatiently. Frank just grunted. Neither of them was interested in anything she might have to say, in anything that might interest her. She was not one of them. She had arrived too late.

She could not mention the telescope. 'Oh, someone at school said there was a park or something up there. Some old ruins,' she hazarded. She had not taken it in at the time, but the more she thought about what she had seen the more certain she was that somewhere in the picture there had been grey stonework, a narrow pointed window.

'There's no park up there; you know where the park is,' Helen said, adding, inevitably, 'and you're not to go up there on your own.'

'Golf course,' Frank said finally. 'There's a golf course. That's grass, isn't it?'

'Have we got a map?'

'Of course we've got maps,' Helen said. 'But you know what Mum says, stay on the estate.'

'You taking up golf, man?' Frank ambled out of the kitchen, no doubt going to bed now that everyone else was up.

Grace went back into the office and climbed on the desk to reach the bookcase. Anyone would think that across the Sittingbourne Road lay bandit country. It was scarcely four hundred metres away, in a straight line, but as far as she could recall, she had never crossed it.

The maps were on the top shelf of the bookcase

and most of them were very old, dating back to the times when cars were rarer on the roads than horses; maps that had been made before ring roads and bypasses and clover-leaf flyovers. A lot of them were maps of the same areas and, under Dad's supervision, Grace liked to lay them out and see how those places had looked in 1908, 1939, 1967, watching towns grow and engulf villages, railways vanish, lanes become roads, roads become motorways.

The map she found was too early to show the estate but she located Sittingbourne Road without any trouble, running from lower left to upper right, with Wing Farm to the south of it, the narrow lane which was now Wing Farm Drive and, leading from it, the old cart track that had become Nettlefield Close. The bus depot was already there, and the end of the cart track was also the end of the Close, so all she had to do was imagine a straight line from where the Milners' house now stood, through the bus depot. What lay at the end of it? Frank had been right, it was the golf course.

She was just about to investigate the hinterland of the golf course when she noticed that a pair of feet had walked in and was now standing at the edge of the map. She did not even have to look up to see who owned the feet, for a voice said, 'And what do you think you're up to?'

'I was just looking for something.' She began hurriedly to fold the map.

'You know perfectly well that you're not to touch those on your own, especially the old ones.'

'I didn't think you'd mind,' Grace said, adding silently, Well, you weren't here to ask, were you? She was folding the map the wrong way, out of nervousness, and it was beginning to bunch.

'Why?' Dad said, meaning, Why did you think I wouldn't mind? He took the map away from her and folded it right side in. '*This* is why I mind.'

'I was just looking for something quickly. I wasn't going to be long.'

'It doesn't take long to damage something.' He had never recovered from finding Frank with a biro, some years ago, adding the M20 to a nineteenth-century map of mid-Kent. 'Now, what were you looking for?'

Dad was never cross for longer than it took him to let you know he was cross, but Grace did not know how cross he would be if he found out about the telescope.

'Someone said there were old ruins near here – I was just looking –'

'What sort of old ruins?' Dad slipped the map back into its file and returned it to the bookcase.

'A castle.'

'Like Coldrum?' He meant the collapsed stone barrow at the foot of the downs.

'I don't think so.' Coldrum Castle was older than any knight in armour. A ghost that wandered out of Coldrum would most likely be wearing skins. 'Sort of – of – like when there were knights.'

'There were knights around for hundreds of years. Anybody who went to war on a horse was a knight. These days you get knighted for running a biscuit factory, but in the old days a man who could afford to fight on horseback was a knight.'

'Afford? I thought everybody had horses then.'

'What do you mean, *then*?' Dad was happy again. He loved explaining things, preferably machinery, but apparently he knew about knights too. 'You couldn't get on just any old horse and go to war. You're thinking of the Middle Ages, aren't you? Say fourteenth century. Most of the soldiers were infantry, fighting on foot, with bows; longbows, if they were English. English longbowmen were the best in the world.'

Grace, although interested, was afraid he would wander off the subject of knights and start talking about archers. 'They didn't have horses?'

'A longbow was as tall as a man. How could you shoot that from a horse? You're thinking of cowboys and Indians. No, the knight was a one-man tank, mobile, covered in armour. His horses had to be bred specially, great strong stallions, sixteen hands high, some of them. Destriers, they were called. Don't know why; maybe it means destroyer. And, of course, he had to pay for his own armour and that had to be tailor-made, to fit *him*. All done by hand. And then there was his sword. Being a knight was an expensive business. No such thing as a poor knight – well, actually there was, but a poor knight was a bad knight, probably a soldier of fortune.'

'What's that?' Grace thought it sounded rather dashing.

'A mercenary. Soldier of fortune sounds better,

but a mercenary was what he was. A soldier who fights for money.'

'Soldiers get paid,' Grace said. 'Don't they?'

'Of course they do, but a regular army fights for its country. A mercenary will fight for anyone who pays him. He might even fight *against* his own country if the money was right.'

'Did knights ever fight on foot?'

'If they fell off their horses they had to. Oh yes, when they used their swords they were usually on foot. Anyway, what's all this sudden interest in knights?'

'I was asking about ruins, castles. If there were any near here.'

'Not so far as I know. Now listen, young Auntie.' Dad turned serious. 'If you find any old ruins, stay out of them, all right? Don't go exploring anywhere on your own. And stay on the estate. We've told you that often enough.'

'Can I see if I can find any? Just look?'

'Of course you can look.' Dad evidently thought she was playing some kind of make-believe game if he imagined she was going to look for ruins on a council estate. 'No harm in looking. But you're never to go anywhere without telling somebody first.' He turned to his mail. 'Now, let's see what we've got here . . .'

Grace left him frowning over the letters and went back to the kitchen. It was empty. Mum was already out shopping, Frank had gone to bed and Helen was almost certainly back in her room, putting on her face before she went to work. If Grace went up there she would be made to feel an intruder, even though it was her room too. Why couldn't Frank get a job, or go to university, or become a New-Age traveller, something that would entail his leaving home? Then she and Helen could have a room each. At least Helen would be away for months at a time next year; could she bear to wait that long? If only Mum and Dad would buy their house, like the Milners had. Then they could put in a loft extension too.

She could imagine herself in it. The estate was built on a slope, so her house was higher up than the Milners'. From the loft she might be able to see over their roof, with all the view that Steffi had and perhaps a little more, and with all the time in the world to find the trees and the lawn, the place where her knight had walked among the white waiting people.

If only she hadn't said anything about looking for ruins. All it had done was make Dad tell her over again not to go anywhere on her own and not to go off the estate. If he had not repeated it only minutes ago, she might have been tempted to pretend she had forgotten since last time.

Which was yesterday morning. 'The world's a dangerous place, these days,' Mum had said. 'Anything can happen. Anyway, it's not just you, is it? How many of your friends are allowed to wander about by themselves?'

Someone was rapping on the back door. Grace recognized Steffi's outline through the frosted glass and went to open it. Steffi shoved an envelope into her hand.

'From Dad, for your dad. Something about the low-loader, for the rally.' She turned to go.

'Wait.' Grace pawed at her arm and missed, but Steffi swung round as if Grace had hit her.

'Now what?'

'Can I come over and look out your window again?'

'Not allowed up there,' Steffi said. 'Sorry.'

'No, not the loft. Your bedroom.' You could see the very top of the hill, even from lower down. 'I just –'

'You just want to poke your nose in,' Steffi said. 'Mind your own business.'

'No, really, it's something I saw last night –'

'I said no.' Steffi's eyebrows drew into a hard, straight line, parallel with her hard, straight mouth. 'And don't start hanging round me again. Go and play with your Tiny Tears.'

Grace knew better than to retort that she had not played with dolls for years. Steffi would only think of something worse, more withering, like 'What's the matter with you? Nappy rash?'

Here was more proof, as if she needed it, that no one really cared about her. Very well, if nobody would help her she would have to help herself. 'Don't go off the estate,' they all said. 'Don't go anywhere on your own.' Which meant, if you looked at it carefully, don't go off the estate on your own. Which meant perhaps, that it might be all right to go with a friend.

It did not mean that at all, and it would not be all right. But who would know?

Chapter Four

'**A**untie! Where do you think you're off to?' Mum, who had radar scanners for ears, looked out of the kitchen as Grace walked quietly along the hall.

'Just down to Lucy's.'

'Why are you sneaking out the front, then?'

'Just getting my *coat*,' Grace said, getting it. 'I thought it might *rain*.'

'Be back by four,' Mum said, and went on raking damp clothes out of the washing machine. She never took her own washing to the launderette.

'Why?' Grace said.

'Because I say so,' Mum replied, which was no answer at all, Grace considered. Now that she could no longer be accused of sneaking she walked out of the front door anyway, to avoid getting into a conversation. In a few seconds Mum might say something else, assuming that Grace was still within earshot. She closed the door very quietly.

Hammering sounds came from the garage, where Frank and Salvo were working on the Fordson. Salvo had arrived at half-past one, so it was probably about two o'clock now. The battery in Grace's watch had run flat a week ago, although she was still wearing it, with the hands still at twenty-past three. It could not possibly be twenty-past three yet. Say two o'clock, then; that gave her two hours; it ought to be plenty of time to walk up the hill and find what she was looking for.

She was not at all sure exactly what she *was* looking for. In her mind's eye she still carried the image of the two poplars, the railings, the traffic signal, burned on her memory as if she had looked too long at a light bulb. In addition, she now had a map. It was drawn from memory on three sheets of the small pink writing paper that Helen had given her on her ninth birthday. She had not yet written enough letters to use it up. The bunch of flowers printed on each corner had got badly in the way of her mapmaking until she thought of using the backs, but she had been in a hurry to get down what she had seen, or thought she had seen, before Dad had come and taken his own map away.

Grace was almost at Lucy Claggett's house

before she took out the pink sheets and examined them. The road she needed was called Barrack Hill, and as far as she could remember it turned up out of Sittingbourne Road not far from the point where Wing Farm Drive ran down into it. The golf course was very close, on the left (she *knew* it was on the left), so the traffic light ought to be near the top of Barrack Hill. Even if she did not find the knight today she would at least find out where to begin her search. Seriously, she knew that she was not expecting to find the knight patiently hanging about especially for her, but she might find the green lawn where he had walked and that place where the white figures had stood. Had the white figures vanished when the knight vanished, or had they just become invisible as the sun stopped shining? Almost they were more mysterious than the knight himself, if he *was* a knight. Whatever else she had imagined, she had not imagined a horse.

She could see into the Claggetts' front room from the garden path. Lucy was sprawled on the settee in front of the television, looking bored, and when Grace knocked she saw her leap up eagerly to answer. However, she did not open the door but came to the window and fumbled with the lock and catch.

'D'you want to come in?' Lucy said, when she saw who it was. 'I've got some new videos.'

'I'm going for a walk,' Grace said. 'Do you want to come?'

'A *walk*?' Lucy managed to make this sound as exotic as wrestling with a python. Perhaps it was, to Lucy, who was driven everywhere by her mum, even the half-mile to school. Grace hardly ever went for walks either. Come to think of it, nobody did unless they had a dog.

'Where?' Lucy said wonderingly.

'Across Sittingbourne Road.' This was like crossing the Channel, judging by Lucy's expression. 'The people over the road from us have got a room in the loft and I was looking out of the window and –' she edited out the telescope, that was too risky. People talked, '– and you can see all these things that aren't there when you're lower down. I just wanted to go and look.'

'What do you mean, aren't there?'

'I mean I never knew they were there till I saw them.' Or maybe they aren't there at all . . .

'What things?'

'Well, fields and houses and that.' She would not let on that she was going in search of something that *really* wasn't there; Lucy wasn't that much of a friend.

Lucy, evidently not at all enthralled by the prospect of climbing a hill on a hot afternoon to see fields and houses, was beginning to withdraw again. 'Whyn't you come in? I'll show you my new matching top and leggings.'

'We might be able to see for miles when we get to the top. It won't take long. It looks ever so nice up there.'

Lucy swung on the window.

'All right. I'll put proper shoes on. Just a minute.'

There was more scrabbling with locks and bolts behind the door and Lucy came out wearing a jacket and shoes. Grace eyed the shoes doubtfully. They were shiny and thin, not the best sort for walking in, but she could hardly tell Lucy what to wear. She also had an umbrella, the kind that telescoped into itself until it was about the size of a winter cucumber.

'Might rain,' Lucy said, looking prudently at the sky. 'Mum gets really ratty if I get my hair wet, you know, in case I get that ear infection again like I had when we were doing the nativity play, you remember, and I had all guck coming out of it on the pillow and my hair stuck to the sheet.' Lucy was going to grow up to be one of those people who sat behind you in the bus, describing operations.

Crossing the Sittingbourne Road was not like crossing the Channel, more like fording a river in spate. It was so wide and busy that there were little islands in the middle where you could rest up for the next sprint.

'Mum doesn't like me crossing here,' Lucy said primly, as Grace clutched her sleeve and ran for the nearest island. 'If I'd have got run over then it would have been your fault.'

This was true but it hardly needed saying, Grace thought. She decided not to mind, and seeing that the traffic was slowing down for the lights where they ought to have crossed, she urged Lucy towards the opposite pavement.

'What's all these bits of paper?' Lucy said, as Grace struggled to control her maps in the gusty draught from a passing lorry.

'It's the way we're going,' Grace said, holding them out.

'They're a bit messy, aren't they?'

That did not need saying either. 'I had to copy them in a hurry,' Grace said, strenuously not minding again. 'Wasn't easy.'

'Why are we going this way? We could have gone up that road by where we crossed.'

'This is the way I worked out,' Grace said. In her head was the increasingly vague memory of the hillside as she had seen it from Steffi's window. It was probably more accurate than the maps, but it was fading fast, like a photograph left too long in the sun. The only street she was sure about was Barrack Hill. Unless they stuck to that they would be lost before they began.

'This is boring,' Lucy complained, about ten metres up Barrack Hill. As Grace had foreseen, they were walking past the back of the bus depot, a long, featureless brick wall.

'It'll be interesting once we get to the top.'

'Walking's boring.' It was like saying that breathing was boring. You had to breathe to stay alive. You had to walk to get anywhere. 'I wish I'd brought my bike.' All right, you had to walk if you didn't have wheels. Grace's bike had never recovered from being borrowed by Frank for his paper round.

'It's all uphill,' Lucy was droning.

'It'll be downhill coming back. Anyway, uphill's worse on a bike.'

On her map Grace had drawn Barrack Hill as a straight line, but in fact it was turning, starting to go downhill again. Almost opposite a road led out of it, a road that was still going up, although not very steeply.

'Along there,' Grace said.

'Why?'

'The place I want to get to is near the top.'

'Oh. You didn't say we were going to a *place*.'

'I don't know. I'm only trying to find it —'

'Does X mark the spot?' Lucy made a grab at the maps again. 'I'm surprised you can find anything on here.'

'It was just somewhere that looked nice and I wanted to see it.' If only she could have gone alone. Lucy whingeing at her side made her feel as if she were carrying a bag of heavy shopping.

Now this road was turning too, on its way down again. It had not been apparent from Steffi's window that what looked like one hill was made up of several little hills.

'Up here,' Grace said, at the next corner. This street was called Denmark Road and it was going up so steeply that the houses on either side rose in steps, each front door higher than the next. Lucy began to breathe heavily. Perhaps her feet hurt in those slippy, shiny shoes. Grace hoped she would not start demanding to go back. The streets did not look a bit as they had done from the loft window, and nothing like the lines on her map. She was not even sure if she would be able to find Sittingbourne Road again.

Denmark Road turned at a right angle and then, Grace noted fatalistically, started going downhill. There was a big white house at the corner, with a poplar in the garden, but it was only one poplar and there were no traffic lights.

'Along here,' Grace said, turning right past the

big white house. Lucy followed but she was beginning to limp. Grace could not tell if it were a real limp or a protest limp, but she did not want to ask about it and let herself in for one of Lucy's septic explanations. There was something familiar about the big white house on the corner of Denmark Road, and when she looked ahead and saw a filling station at the far end, she knew where they were. This was the street that Steffi and Sarah had been looking for through the telescope; there was the corner house, halfway down, that they had been spying on. Now she remembered; the street by that house went uphill towards the place where the traffic light was.

'It's all right, I know where we are,' she started to say, but they were just drawing level with the corner house, and as they reached the corner itself, down the road came two girls on bicycles. They were not just any two girls, either. They were Steffi and Sarah.

Grace began to feel guilty even before Steffi recognized her. She had as much right to be walking around this particular corner as Steffi had to be riding round it, but she had a premonition that Steffi would not see it this way. Steffi leapt from her bike while it was still moving and stormed across the road. Sarah, who had not recognized Grace, possibly because she never bothered to look at her, carried on round the corner and was well into Denmark Road before she looked back and saw what was happening.

'Are you following me?' Steffi shrieked, snatching Grace by the arm. 'What are you doing here? Who asked you to come poking your nose in?'

Lucy backed up against a wall, eyes and mouth wide open. Sarah slewed round on her bike and came back.

'It's her with the telescope. What's she doing here?'

'That's what I want to know. Well?' Steffi brought her face down close to Grace's and began prodding her shoulder. 'Well? *Well?*'

'We're just going for a walk,' Grace said, trying to twist away from Steffi. 'I wasn't following you. Why should I? I didn't know you'd be here.'

'Oh, yeah? 'Course you didn't.' Steffi's jabs were becoming punches, hard and painful. Grace, although she had known that Steffi would be annoyed, because she always was, had never thought that she would completely lose her rag. The punches hurt. Grace shrank into her jacket as Steffi grabbed her on either side of her neck and began to shake her. Sarah, left with nothing to do, went for Lucy.

'What are you gawping at?'

Lucy's mouth, already conveniently open, let out a squeal of fright. 'I'm going home. I'll tell my mum you got me into a fight.'

There was a sudden scuffle. Sarah and Lucy collided and bounced apart as Lucy, remembering that she was armed, pressed the spring on her umbrella, which opened explosively. Sarah turned on Grace as Lucy fled, the umbrella juddering over her head, back up Denmark Road to home and safety. Without looking where she was going she stepped into the road and a car, slowing down to make the turn, swerved round her and ran over the front wheel of Steffi's bicycle which was still lying in the gutter.

'Now look what you've done!' Steffi screamed, letting go of Grace with a final clout. The car stopped and the driver got out. He and Steffi and Sarah converged upon the injured bicycle and Grace was forgotten. She ran.

It was only when she stopped, out of breath, that she realized that instead of following Lucy she had taken the road up past the corner house that Steffi was so interested in. Somewhere in her flight she had turned another corner. When she looked back there was no sign of Sarah, Steffi, the car or the bicycles. Everywhere she looked were houses, identical semi-detached houses with steep tiled roofs sharing a central chimney stack. Between each pair of houses was a pair of garages. In front were low brick walls. Grace stared all round. The houses seemed to shrug and move closer together, closer to her.

This street ran neither up hill nor down. Grace walked back a few paces but she could not even find the turning that had led her there, as though the houses really had closed up around her to cut off her retreat. Over the tops of the roofs she could see more roofs, and another row beyond that. So this long level road must run *across* the hill. She sat down on one of the walls and looked at her maps. Could this be Sandringham Drive, Windsor Crescent? It was too straight to be a crescent; Buckingham Gardens? Balmoral Avenue?

Grace looked each way along the road. At the back of her mind a sensible voice told her that she was not really lost; that in a straight line she could not be more than twenty minutes from home; that the roofs of the houses all around her were the roofs that she had seen from Steffi's loft; but it was no comfort. Why were there no people about?

Because it's Saturday afternoon and they're all watching sport on telly, said the sensible voice, but she took no notice. *Knock on a door and ask for directions*, the voice went on. But hadn't she been told over and over not to go to the houses of strangers? Dare she speak if someone finally did appear?

Without caring which way she was going, Grace began to walk along the street the way that she had been running. If the sun were out she would know that it ought to be on her left or behind her, but the clouds were thickening. *If you come to a street going downhill you'll get back to the Sittingbourne Road*, said the sensible voice, but when she came to a turning that led uphill she took it. The afternoon was growing darker. At last she did see a few cars and one or two people, but they seemed unreal in the greenish light, as if they would not see her or hear her if she spoke to them. And then the road curved ahead of her, there was a junction and a set of traffic signals. On the far side of the road were railings, grass and trees – fir trees, chestnut trees, a mountain ash with scarlet berries and two tall poplars. She began to run again.

At the junction she stopped and looked to her left where the road ran downhill. At the foot were more trees but beyond them were three long roofs – the bus depot – allotments, a row of houses which must be Nettlefield Close. She could even see the new window in the roof of the last one: Steffi's.

Now that she knew where she was Grace could allow herself to wonder about the time. Her watch, naturally, still said twenty-past three and by now it might very well *be* twenty-past three. She had no idea how long she had been out. If she got home late there would be a row, but there might be a row anyway if Lucy had done what she had threatened to do and told Mum about the fight.

Wasn't my fault, Grace reasoned. Wasn't a fight; it was bullying. But Mum would never believe that Steffi could be a bully. In any case, how could she go back now, when she had walked so far and suffered so much? now that she was on the verge of finding what she had come searching for? She waited until the lights changed and crossed the road.

The grass behind the railings was the golf course. There was a sign to prove it, beside a padlocked iron gate, but next to the gate was a stile and a finger post which said *Public Footpath*.

Between the golf course and the footpath stood a high hedge of clipped evergreens that let no light through, and on the other side of the path was a high boarded fence. The path itself was damp and mossy and so dark that it seemed to run through a tunnel. Once over the stile Grace kept looking back to see if there was anyone following her, wondering what she would do if there was, or if she met somebody coming the other way. It was the kind of place that she had been warned to stay away from. Anyone who hung around a place like this must be up to no good – except for her, of course.

On her right the fence was replaced by a low holly hedge with a gate in it. A long lawn with fruit trees sloped upward to the back of a house; a house, Grace estimated rapidly, that must be as big as the whole block of four that she lived in. This garden was like a park; could it be the place that she had seen through the telescope? No; on the left the evergreen hedge was still looming over her. When she found the place she would know it because she would also be able to see Steffi's window. She moved on. The holly hedge became a high fence again, but the evergreens suddenly ended and gave place to a brick wall. The path was lighter here but she could see that up ahead trees met over it and turned it into a real tunnel.

The wall stopped at a buttress with a stone ball on top, and on her left now was a strip of rough grass with thorny bushes sprouting from it. This too was the sort of place she was warned to avoid, but beyond the bushes were trees and through a gap she saw again the roofs of the bus depot, the allotments, the Close. There was Steffi's window. Grace turned her head. On the other side of the path were railings with spear heads, oak trees and dark yews, and among the trees, silent motionless white figures, row upon row. She knew at once what she was looking at, but the knowledge did not reassure her; it was a graveyard.

These were the figures she had seen through the telescope, waiting in lines on the hillside, so the next open space must be the place where the knight had appeared. She began to move more quickly, slithering a little on the muddy path. The grave-yard was bounded by a stone wall, and on the far side of that the railings changed to chestnut stakes. There was a stretch of lawn behind the palings, rose bushes, apple trees, and a brick building – not a house, although it had windows, one upstairs, one down. The house lay farther back, past the apple trees, but in the brick building a light was showing. The windows were dirty and the upper one, where the light glowed faintly, was whitewashed.

Grace edged along the palings until she was level with the downstairs window. It was dark in the tunnel of trees and even darker inside the building, but through the window she could just make out a huge, overhanging shape, two metres high at least, like a gigantic hand with the thumb and forefinger closed to make a circle. She leaned as far as she could across the palings to see better, and a movement overhead made her look up.

In the gloom the whitewashed window glim-mered, and at the bottom, just above the sill, a dark mass was slowly rising behind it, inexorably upward, until it filled the window and resolved itself into a head, shoulders, arms, legs, a whole human shadow hovering in the window and coming towards her. Grace did not wait for it to pass through the glass and float out over the paling fence. She turned back the way she had come and fled.

It began to rain as she neared the end of the footpath; great hard drops slammed on to the moss and mud, and by the time she reached the stile she was skating instead of running. It was almost as dark out in the open now as it had been on the footpath. Looking down the hill she saw a ragged strip of light between the clouds and the horizon, but the sky overhead was the colour of old bruises. Thunder growled discontentedly in the distance.

Never stand under trees during a thunderstorm. Grace moved away from the stile out of habit. She was not afraid of thunder or lightning. After what she had just witnessed she doubted if there was anything left on earth, or off it, with the power to frighten her. That dreadful silhouette slowly advancing to the window was far more terrifying than the knight in the telescope, than the brooding graveyard, than the risk of being struck by lightning.

But she knew that sooner or later she would have to go back because, even in her terror, she had recognized that other massive overhanging shape behind the window in the dusky lower room. She had seen a wheeling machine.

Chapter Five

*T*he rain came down in hard straight lines, and came down and down, like an endless bead curtain. Grace almost regretted losing Lucy and the umbrella although she knew that if Lucy had stayed with her they would never have got as far as the traffic lights even. There was no shelter away from the trees and within two minutes she was as wet as she could be, with water bubbling in her shoes until she felt as if her feet were dissolving. She followed the railings downward, keeping her eyes fixed on the rapidly widening strip of light on the horizon. She could even see sunlight glinting on distant roofs but it would be a long while before the sun came anywhere near where she was.

Halfway down the hill stood a bus stop and a telephone box. As well as all her warnings another of Mum's precautions was to insist that Grace always kept a ten-pence piece in her pocket for emergencies. This did not feel like an emergency to Grace, but she still did not know what the time was. It might very well have become an emergency at home.

She went into the phone box, which was the open kind, offering no shelter at all, and rang home. Usually the Lincoln honked for ages before anyone answered it, unless Dad was in, being Hon. Sec., but this time it was lifted at once − a bad sign. People hung about near phones only if they were anxious.

'Hullo?'

'*Salvo?*'

'Is that you, Auntie?'

He sounded worried.

'What's the matter?'

'What's the matter, she says.' Salvo's voice relaxed a little. 'Listen, you better get your ass back here but *fast*, man. There's a posse out looking for you.'

'What do you mean, a posse?'

'Frank, for a start. Your mum, your dad −'

'What's the time?'

'Nearly half-past five. Where you been, Auntie? Your friend Lucy's mum come around here −'

'I'll be home in ten minutes. Tell them I'm all right if they get back first.'

'Is that the truth, man? No one holding a gun to your head?'

'No, really. I'm nearly home now.'

He hung up. She had said that only to reassure him, but the rain was easing off and at the foot of the hill she could see heavy traffic passing. That must be Sittingbourne Road, and the road she was on must be the one she had seen on Dad's map, that she had mistaken for Barrack Hill.

The sun was out by the time she reached the end of the Close, and over Barrack Hill a brilliant rainbow hung against the clouds. Grace did not pause to admire it. Looking up the Close she could see something far more threatening than thunder clouds: Mum, standing in the road waiting for her, with Wendy Milner and Steffi at the edge of their garden. Everyone looked upset – well, Wendy looked upset. Mum looked frightened and furious. Steffi looked as if she would sink her teeth into the first person who came close enough.

No one said anything. Mum waited until she had come right up to them before she said, 'Inside.'

That was all. Grace opened her mouth, not to try and explain, just to say sorry, but it was no use.

'Inside.'

She went and stood in the kitchen, afraid to move any farther, even to fetch a towel to dry her hair. Water ran off her clothes and out of her shoes. She stared at the floor and watched the drops become blobs and the blobs merge into pools, waiting for what seemed like twenty minutes but was probably twenty seconds, until she heard

Mum come in behind her and close the door. Mum had not shouted at her and she shut the door quietly; that proved how angry she was. Grace was afraid to turn her head. Mum hardly ever slapped her, but she was sure she was going to do it now. She got ready for the blow, shoulders tensed.

'Your dad's out looking for you,' Mum said. 'In all that rain. And Frank. And I was. I only just got back. I was going to call the police.'

Grace went on looking at the floor. The pools were meeting round her feet in a kind of ox-bow lake.

'Mrs Claggett came round. She said Lucy told her you'd been in a fight with Steffi; said you ran off and left her. *Three hours ago.* Where've you been?'

'I never ran off and left her,' Grace said. 'She left *me*. And I wasn't fighting Steffi. Steffi hit me. I only ran to get away from her. I got lost.'

'Yes, you got lost because you were off over the road, weren't you? Where I've told you not to go I don't know how many times. Stay on the estate, I said, and what do you do? Go straight off and disobey me, and look what happens −'

They were still standing in the middle of the kitchen, one in front of the other, Grace with her back to Mum. She dared not look round. Mum was crying.

'Don't you ever listen to what I tell you? I've said you're *never* to go off the estate. Where have you been? Who've you been *with*?'

The door to the hall opened and Salvo slipped in.

'Jacquie, she soak to the bone,' he said softly. 'Let her get changed, eh? I'll put the kettle on. Come on, you sit down. Auntie, go dry yourself off.'

Grace went without looking back. Mum did not answer, but she heard a chair scrape on the floor, the tap running. Salvo seemed to be taking charge. Salvo had waited by the phone in case she called, and now he was there being fatherly with Mum. She longed to tell him about the wheeling machine; or would it be better to wait until she was sure that she had not imagined that as well?

It was, she decided as she took off her sodden clothes in the bathroom, getting harder and harder to believe the things she was seeing: the knight, the shadow – oh, the shadow – and the wheeling machine. What else could it have been? She had glimpsed it only for a moment but it was exactly like the one in the picture that Frank had shown her. She would have to go back and make certain. The biggest problem would be persuading Mum ever to let her go anywhere ever again. She was sure to be grounded after this.

She tiptoed across the landing to her room, but there was no sound from downstairs. It was so unfair. When she was little Frank and Helen were out all the time; she was sure of that because they were never around to play with her. She would have remembered if there had ever been this kind of fuss about *them* being late. And it was only an hour and a half late, in broad daylight. She hadn't gone out deliberately to get lost. She had even gone with Lucy, useless Lucy, so as not to be alone.

She put on dry clothes, combed out her hair and went downstairs. The kitchen door was slightly open and Grace looked round it. Mum was alone at the table with the mug of tea that Salvo had made her. Another mug stood on the far side, faintly steaming.

'That's for you,' Mum said. 'You don't deserve it,' she added predictably. 'Salvo made it. Now he's out sweet-talking the others.'

'Sweet-talking?'

'That's what he calls it,' Mum said. 'I'd call it soft-soaping. Now, tell me what happened.'

Grace wished that she could tell her everything, starting with Steffi's loft, but that would involve the telescope. Even if she were forgiven for this afternoon she did not care to risk asking for other offences to be taken into consideration.

'I just wanted to go for a walk,' she said.

'There's plenty of places to walk round here.'

'I've *been* everywhere round here. You always say don't go off the estate, but there's nothing to do. *Why* can't I go off the estate? Frank and Helen used to go all over the place. I bet Lynette and Gavin and Alison went all over the place when they were kids. You never let me go anywhere.'

'I let you go to Brownies. It's not my fault you didn't like it.'

'I suppose I should've liked it because it was the only place I could go.'

'Don't push your luck,' Mum warned her. 'You're in trouble – big trouble.'

65

'Sorry,' Grace mumbled. 'Really I'm sorry. I never meant to worry you. It was only an hour and a half.'

'Half a minute is all it would take.' Mum said.

'What would?'

'Look, Auntie, *think*. Why don't we let you go where you like? Because it's not safe, that's why. I know the others used to wander all over the place, but that was different. It was a long while ago. It isn't safe any more. Times have changed.'

'How?' Grace said.

'Don't you ever watch the news, read the papers? There's kids like you, older than you, go missing every day; abducted, murdered, never seen again. There's that man in court now —'

'I wouldn't go with anyone,' Grace said. 'Never. You know I wouldn't. I never get lifts or go in people's houses.'

'You wouldn't have to go. You might be taken. That's why we always want you with someone.'

'When till?' Grace said. 'Till I'm grown up?'

'Till we can trust you.'

'You *can* trust me.'

'Like this afternoon?'

'I was all right. I just got lost.'

'But where were you?'

'Just over Sittingbourne Road, just walking about. It's nice over there.'

At the time, she had to confess privately, she had not thought it at all nice, but even Mum would have to admit that the streets on Barrack Hill were nicer than the estate. She had not seen a single house with a fifty-year-old coal lorry standing in the drive, for a start.

'There's houses up there with huge gardens, like parks, and the golf course —'

'You stay off that golf course.'

'Why? Because it's private? I know that.'

'Because someone got done in there, that's why.'

Grace thought of the shadow. 'I wouldn't go anywhere like that.' She thought of the footpath, silent, deserted, deeply secluded; the scrubby grassland, the graveyard . . . all the kinds of places that Mum was afraid of. 'Well, it would have been all right if Lucy hadn't run off like that. I mean, if Steffi hadn't started thumping me —'

'Yes, and why did Steffi start thumping you?'

'She thought we were following her. We weren't. She was coming the other way.'

'That Lucy's such a drip . . .' Mum said. 'What good would she have been if you were attacked?'

'We *were* attacked.'

'See what I mean?' Mum said. 'You got jumped by a couple of thirteen-year-olds, and what did you do? Panic and get lost. No, sorry love, you can't be trusted and I'm grounding you. I don't know what your dad'll have in mind. And when we let you out again, stay on the estate. And if you go off on your own, and I find out — and I *will* find out — you won't just be grounded. Do you understand?'

Grace nodded.

'So just hope and pray Salvo did get round your dad,' Mum said.

*

67

Sweet talk or soft soap, Salvo had done the trick. All Dad said when he came in was, 'Another performance like that and you'll *really* cop it.' Grace too was crying by then and he added, 'Look, I might have six but I can't spare even one,' and by the time she had worked out what he meant he had gone again, to have a hot bath.

She had cried because she saw at last that they had all been as frightened as she had been, but of something that might really have happened, not, like her, of something that could not possibly be happening. The fuss and the fright, the row with Mum, had driven to the edge of her mind the sight of the dreadful hovering shadow in the whitewashed window, but it had continued to hover, out of sight. Later, when she lay in bed, alone in the dark, it surged forward again. If she looked out from under the quilt it might be in the room, having followed her home.

It was strange, but the more evidence she had, first the knight, then the shadow, that there was something odd going on up there on the hill, the harder it was to believe it. It was much easier to believe in things that other people had told her: tales of apparitions that someone's granny had seen, inexplicable noises that someone's uncle had heard, things that happened to neighbours, that were kept safely at a distance because they had involved not a friend, but the friend of a friend. If she said to someone, '*I* saw the ghost of a knight in armour. *I* saw a shadow that floated out of a window,' no one would believe her.

She pushed the quilt down over her shoulder

and looked boldly round the room. There were no shadows that should not have been there. After the rain storm it was a windless night. Nothing moved on walls or ceiling, no phantom outline hung in the dark air. But then, she thought, the things that she had seen did not belong to the night; they appeared in the daytime, daylight phantoms that had nothing to hide. By daylight she must go and look for them again and confront them, because unless she did she would never be sure about the wheeling machine.

She was so tired that when Helen came in she never woke, and in the morning she had to look twice at Helen's bed to make sure that she was in it. Helen slept on her back, flat, like a corpse. Grace was very quiet getting up because if she disturbed Helen the corpse would sit up and throw things, usually shoes, once the alarm clock. She dressed in the bathroom.

Frank, unusually, was already up when she came downstairs. She could hear a power tool whining in the garage and it could not be Dad because Dad was in the hall, making Hon. Sec. calls to a colleague.

'Where's Mum?'

'Over at Gavin and Rachel's. Don't you go out of the garden, right?'

'Right,' Grace muttered. She slouched into the kitchen and put some bread in the toaster. They thought that by forgiving her everything was made all right again. Well, it was, for them. They were all carrying on as usual, Helen sleeping, Frank working on the lorry, Dad being Hon. Sec., Mum over at Gavin's giving Rachel a hand because the baby was nearly due. And no one had to waste a second worrying about her because she was grounded. No one wasted a second thinking about what that actually meant to *her*.

The bread sprang out of the toaster. Grace piled marmalade on the two slices and went out to the garage with one for herself and one for Frank, as a peace offering. As she came through the side gate she could not help looking up, and saw Steffi glaring down from the open skylight. Mum and Dad might have forgiven her but Steffi had not. Steffi had been hauled across by Wendy last night to say that she was sorry, although it was plain to see that the only thing she felt sorry about was having to say so.

Frank was at the back of the garage, in the shadow of the Fordson, drilling holes in a sheet of metal.

'Huh, you didn't get murdered then,' was all he said when he saw her. 'Get out of our light, Auntie.'

'Murdered? No, I'm grounded though.'

'Didn't mean that,' Frank said, raising his voice to be heard above the drill. 'Mum thought someone had got you yesterday. If I'd found you first you *would* have been murdered. Ruined my trainers.'

'Sorry,' Grace said, knowing that Frank must have been worried too or he would never have gone out into the storm in his Nikes, which were almost new. Grace had seen them only just now, drying off in the airing cupboard.

'Didn't you ever come home late when you were young?'

'It was different for me.' The sound of the drill died away. Frank looked round and she handed him the toast.

'Because you're a boy?'

'No; because there weren't so many nutters around then, I suppose.'

'Most people don't get murdered,' Grace said.

'It's not me that grounded you,' Frank said. He was sympathetic, she could see but, being Frank, it would never occur to him on his own to do anything about it.

'Would you go for a walk with me?'

'*What?*'

She might have been asking him to take her skiing.

'A walk. They wouldn't mind if you went with me.'

She watched him honestly trying ·to imagine himself, Frank Thompson, taking his little sister for a walk. Evidently he failed.

'Don't be daft, Auntie,' he said.

'It wouldn't be far, not for long. There's something I want to see.'

She wondered whether to tell him about the wheeling machine, but it would be such a disappointment if it turned out to be as imaginary as the knight and the shadow – well, not imaginary, that was not quite the word she was searching for.

'I'll think about it,' Frank was saying.

'When?'

'I'm already thinking. Don't *hassle* me, Auntie – and look where you're treading!'

Grace's feet had become entangled with a twisted length of steel.

'What is it?'

'A rear mudguard. Meant to be,' Frank said sadly, as Grace went out.

Helen's corpse had resurrected itself and was sitting at the kitchen table staring at a bowl of cornflakes. Helen had missed everything yesterday, but somebody must have told her. She looked up sourly when Grace walked in.

'Been making a nuisance of yourself again?'

'Again?' Grace said.

'Everybody running around in circles looking for you.'

'They didn't have to,' Grace said.

'Oh, I suppose you'd like it if nobody noticed whether you were missing or not. What happens? *I* get a rocket when I come home because once she starts worrying about *you* Mum starts worrying about *me*. It was only twelve-thirty and everybody was up waiting.'

'I just went for a walk,' Grace said. 'I went out with Lucy Claggett but Steffi and her mate started knocking me about and Lucy ran off. Then her mum comes round here saying I'd got her into a fight. It's all Steffi's fault.'

'It's your own fault. You've been told to stay on the estate.'

'I bet you never had to stay on the estate when you were my age. I didn't want to go with Lucy anyway, but there wasn't anyone else. Will you come for a walk with me?'

'You're grounded.'

'When I'm not grounded.'

'Get real,' Helen said. 'A *walk*?'

'Just up to the golf course.'

'Get realler.'

The morning dragged on. Dad stayed in the office, Frank stayed in the garage and Helen went back to the bedroom to do work for school, which meant that Grace could not go in there. Mum was still at Gavin's.

She might have taken me with her, Grace thought, sulking through the video shelf for something she had not already seen. At half-past twelve Dad called in while she was watching a cartoon and said he was driving over to fetch Mum.

'Can I come too?' Grace sprang up.

'You aren't going anywhere, young lady,' Dad said, not angrily, but finally.

Unfair, unfair. If they'd only tell her how long she was grounded for she could at least look forward to the end of it. Till they could trust her, Mum had said. How was she supposed to know when that would be? Days, weeks? Years? She watched from the window as Dad went out to the car, which had to live in the roadway since the Fordson had arrived, and saw Frank hurry to join him. A minute or two later Helen looked in.

'Was that Dad going out?'

'He's gone to fetch Mum.'

'Damn, I could've got a lift,' Helen said. 'Tell them I'll be back for *EastEnders*. If I'm not, record it. The soap tape's under the *Radio Times*.'

The front door closed. Grace watched Helen strolling down the Close. It was *unbelievably* unfair.

73

They all came and went as they pleased and never gave a thought to what it must be like to have to ask permission every time you wanted to do anything, and then be told you couldn't do it; never thought what it must be like to want to go places and have to ask someone to take you, and then be told they wouldn't. She hated the estate. It was like living on an island. She had been right to think that crossing the Sittingbourne Road was like crossing the Channel. The island was in sight of the mainland, like you could see France from Dover, and the island was dull and boring and miserable while the mainland was mysterious and lovely and full of strange places, but you could only look at it, never go there, because you could not swim. Because you were Auntie, who had arrived too late, and the ferry had sailed.

Chapter Six

Someone in the kitchen was calling, 'Anyone home?'

It was Salvo. He had walked up the Close, past the window, and Grace had not even seen him, she had been so miserable.

'I'm in,' she said, and went out to find him.

Salvo was wearing his plumber's boiler suit so he must be here to work on the Fordson.

'Ah, the lost sheep,' Salvo said, when he saw Grace. 'All your troubles over?'

'No,' said Grace. 'Do you want some coffee?'

'Won't refuse.' Salvo sat down and began to

make a roll-up. 'I thought I got you off the hook, Auntie.'

'Oh, you did,' Grace said. 'I didn't get punished, but I've been grounded. And now everybody's gone out and I haven't got anything to do and I can't go anywhere.'

'Where do you want to go, man?' Salvo said. He lit his rollie and went to stand at the door so as not to fill the kitchen with smoke. 'You sound like you thinking of the moon.'

'I just want to go up the hill, Barrack Hill,' Grace said. 'That's where I went yesterday. There's something up there I want to see – something *you'd* like to see,' she added, struck by a hopeful idea.

'You asking me to take you for a walk, Auntie?' Salvo said. 'Why, I never knew you cared. What will Venetia say?'

'She wouldn't mind, would she?' Grace had not thought about Venetia. Venetia seemed to mind about everything.

'She be frothing at the mouth with jealousy. "That Auntie Thompson, can't keep her hands off my man!"'

The kettle boiled. Grace made two mugs of coffee and they sat on the back step to drink it.

'Now,' Salvo said, 'what's up on that hill that you got to see and I got to see?'

'Can you keep a secret?'

'In my trade,' Salvo said, 'you learn to keep as silent as the grave.'

'What, plumbing?'

'You be surprised. Plumbers learn the innermost

76

secrets of the human house. We get to see what's under the sink.'

'This is a real secret,' Grace said. 'I'd get a real rollicking if anybody found out.'

'I never spill secrets,' Salvo said. His dreads bobbed solemnly. 'I'm not winding you up, Auntie. Tell away.'

'You know we've got a telescope, the one we're not allowed to touch?'

Salvo nodded.

'Well, I did touch it. I borrowed it. Steffi made me, she wanted to look out of her new loft room.'

'That the secret?' Salvo said. 'Hell, Auntie, everybody touch that telescope. Me and Frank, we take it up on the downs at night and watch the stars. We take it down to the town and watch the girls.'

'Does Dad know?'

'Look like we both got a secret,' Salvo said. 'No, he doesn't. But it wouldn't be the end of the world if he found out.'

'It would be the end of the world if he found out *I'd* borrowed it.' Grace was privately very shocked. She had always thought of the telescope as almost holy. But that was the unfairness again. What could Dad do if he found out that Frank and Salvo were borrowing the telescope? Seriously, what *could* he do? 'Anyway,' she said, 'I did borrow it, for Steffi, but I got a look through it too, and I saw something, up on the hill, only I don't think it could be what I thought it was. I've got to find out. That's where I went yesterday.'

'What did you see, a murder? Like in a movie?

You know, *Rear Window* or *The 4.50 from Paddington?*'

'It wasn't anything like that,' Grace said. 'I think I saw a ghost.'

'Through the telescope?'

'Yes. It was a knight in armour. I really did see him, and then yesterday I went and found the place, and it was next to a graveyard, and I saw something else, there was this window, all white-washed, and a shadow, sort of rising up and hovering –'

'Oh my. A shadow, ri-i-i-sing up and ho-ver-ing. I do love jumbie stories.'

'What's jumbie? It's true.'

'Never said it wasn't,' Salvo said. 'Jumbies are ghosts. Look, man, you really truly seen a ghost?'

'Really truly. Well, I really truly saw something, and I don't know what it was if it wasn't a ghost.'

'I think we'll take that little walk, man,' Salvo said dreamily.

'And the other thing . . . you know, I said there was something else that you'd like –'

'What is it?'

'I don't know if I saw that, either.'

They heard a car drawing up outside.

'Can't do it today,' Salvo said, 'but tomorrow maybe, after work.'

Grace scowled at him. 'I thought you meant it.'

'I do mean it, man, but I promised Frank we'd work on the Fordson this afternoon – and you're grounded. Got to get you airborne again, Auntie.'

'More sweet talk?'

'Sweet-sweet talk,' Salvo said. 'Sweet-sweet-sweet.'

But it was Thursday before Salvo's magic worked.

It was worse than living on an island, Grace thought, squatting on the kitchen doorstep where she had sat with Salvo on Sunday, listening to the hiss of compressed air from the garage and smelling the heady tang of paint as Frank and Salvo worked on the cab of the Fordson, so strong it ought to have attracted every solvent-abuser for miles around.

It was like living on an island at war. The house was safe inside its stockade, but beyond the boundary there were land mines and a sniper behind every wall.

The hissing stopped. Grace got ready to jump up, hoping that Salvo would appear round the corner of the garage, bearing good news. She had sworn to herself not to ask him again because that would be hassling, and it would sound as if she hadn't trusted him to keep his promise. She had not hassled Mum and Dad either, so that when Salvo made his move they would have to admit how good she had been about getting grounded, while four perfect rainless days had shone themselves away.

From behind her, in the hall, she heard Helen and her friends going out. Helen had had friends in every day and sometimes during the evening too, which had meant that Grace could not even skulk in her own room. Helen and the friends paused on the path to exchange words with Frank and Salvo, who had come out for fresh air after the painting. All the girls fancied Salvo, except Helen who thought of him as a brother and was therefore about as fond of him as she was of Frank. Salvo did not in the least mind being fancied and leaned on the gatepost soaking up the flirty comments, but he remained true to Venetia, though whether that was out of love, or fear, or laziness, Grace was not sure. Frank draped himself over the opposite gatepost and pointedly refrained from looking up at the Milners' skylight where Sarah Carr had spent the last hour swoon-swooning, under the guise of helping Brian and Steffi with the decorating.

Grace had told Frank about his admirer. 'Perfectly understandable,' said Frank.

Helen and her friends moved off. Frank went back into the garage but Salvo came round to the kitchen door.

'We're clearing up now, man. Give us half an hour and I'll be ready.'

'What for?'

'Don't we have a date?'

'Oh!' Grace cried. 'You mean I can go out?'

'All me powers of persuasion have paid off. Your mum says, just for an hour or two. She thinks I'm mad. So does Frank.'

'What, for going out with me?' Grace felt that it was not entirely tactful of him to say so.

'No, just going for a walk seems like madness to them.'

'But they really said I could?' There was no way of checking up. Mum had just left for work and Dad was off somewhere collecting a load of iron stakes for the rally.

'I told them, "Poor Auntie, pining away for the sight of green fields and hills." No, I tell a lie. Your mum was going to lift the ban tomorrow evening, but I said, "I got to go up to St Dunstan's tonight; can't that suffering child come with me?"'

'Where's St Dunstan's?' Grace said. 'Aren't we going up the hill?'

'Sure we going up it,' Salvo said, 'but that place at the top, where the big houses are, it's called St Dunstan's Green. Kind of a little village only it's joined on to the town now. Got its own shops and school and church.'

The grey stonework, the pointed window; that was what she had seen: a church in a graveyard.

'What are you going up there for?'

'I go up there all the time,' Salvo said, 'with me plunger and me pipe wrench. Plumbers are like the birds of the air, man. We go anywhere.'

'Are you plumbing tonight?'

'Sounds like a song.' He crooned a few bars. '*Are you plumbing tonight? Will you miss me tonight . . .?* No, I'm going up there because Auntie wants to show me something, remember? I'm going to get washed now. Be ready when I call.'

'Off his rocker, man,' Frank said, when he saw Grace in the kitchen, ready to go.

'You can come too.'

'I'm going to clean myself up and stand at the gate to make someone very happy.'

'Sarah? You're not going out with her, are you?'

'What?' Frank looked scandalized. 'She's only a little girl.' Grace wished very much that Sarah and Steffi could have heard that. 'But I don't mind her looking,' said Frank.

'Are you going to tell me what we going to see?' Salvo asked as they turned off Sittingbourne Road, up the hill that Grace had walked down on Sunday through the rain. It was dry now and the sun threw long shadows ahead of them.

'I don't know if it's really there,' Grace said. 'I don't know *what's* there. But if I'm right it'll be a nice surprise.'

'I want to see the apparitions too,' Salvo said. 'I want to see the jumbie knight and the hovering shadow.'

'I really did see them,' Grace said.

'You sure about the knight? Through a telescope? I never heard of seeing a ghost through a telescope.'

'Neither did I,' Grace said. 'He mightn't have been a knight, he didn't have a horse, well, I didn't *see* a horse, but he was in armour. I mean, armour doesn't look like anything else. It was shining and –' A thought struck her. 'What's the time?'

'Ten-past seven. Why?'

'It was quarter-past when I saw him. Sarah said it was ten-past a bit before they let me have the telescope, so it must have been exactly quarter-past, almost.'

82

'Exactly almost,' Salvo said gravely. 'So you think he might appear at the same time each night, like at the moment of his death? Come on, Auntie, get your skates on. We got a date with the risen dead.'

If Grace had been on her own the mere thought of running into the risen dead would have sent her back the way she had come, but with Salvo urging her on she began to trot to keep abreast of him. It was hard work, uphill, but the traffic lights were in sight all the way, and the two poplars, sticking up like rabbit's ears.

'Stop. *Stop*!' Grace shouted as Salvo accelerated past the stile and the mouth of the footpath.

'Down there?' Salvo said. 'Does your mum know you went down there?'

'No.'

'Best she doesn't find out.' He hopped over the stile and Grace followed. 'Weren't you worried, along here, all on your own?'

'Yes,' said Grace, 'but only because of the shadow.'

'I don't know,' Salvo said. 'It's fun to be out on your own, Auntie, exploring and having adventures, but what would you do if someone did make a grab at you, huh?'

'I'd run,' Grace said.

'Yeah, but this is a creepy place, man. This real jumbie territory. Though jumbie'd be the least of your worries if there were nutters about. Don't you come up here on your own again, Auntie.'

'I can't go anywhere,' Grace said. 'That's why I took Lucy with me, only she ran off. Nobody *ever*

83

wants to go anywhere. Nobody's allowed to go anywhere. By the time I'm old enough, I won't want to either.'

'I'm old enough,' Salvo said, 'and I'm here. Hooo! This your graveyard, man?'

'I saw that through the telescope too,' Grace said, 'only I didn't know they were graves. I thought they were people, all in white, standing in rows.'

'Your jumbie knight's jumbie army. Some of them are people,' Salvo said. 'Well, angels. They don't make graves like they used to. This is the back of St Dunstan's Church, Auntie. There's a road on the other side, Rectory Lane.'

They came to the place where the graveyard railings stopped and the paling fence began.

'It was here,' Grace said, and stopped.

'You frightened, man?'

'No.' She was nervous. 'But let's go slowly. That's the building where I saw the shadow. In that window. It just kept coming up, and then it came towards me.'

'The window with the whitewash?'

'Yes. There was a light on.'

'Did it get bigger?' Salvo was staring at the window, unafraid.

She tried to remember. 'No, smaller. I think. It was all shapeless at first, then I saw its head, and an arm.'

'I do hate rational explanations,' Salvo said, 'but I think you saw a real shadow on the white-wash, sort of back projection. Just a person going upstairs with the light behind them. No shadows now, man. And no knight.'

Grace, half disappointed, looked round. Behind her was the open grass, the tree tops and the view right across to the estate, and Steffi's window. The sun was beaming broadly across it all, and the only human shadows in the garden were their own, lying across the lawn where they grew out of the shadows of the palings. The distant house at the top of the garden stood in sunshine, and so did the brick building, both glowing cheerfully.

'Slow ahead,' Salvo whispered, 'softly, softly, not to startle any passing spook.'

Grace stared at it all, the lawn, the fruit trees, the roses; there could be no spooks here; and then she saw something else.

'Salvo!' She gripped his arm and pointed.

The downstairs window of the brick building looked dirtier than ever with the sun shining full upon it. Seeing that, Grace had been ready to steer Salvo to the place where she had leaned across the palings and looked in, but even from where they were standing she could see that now someone was on the other side, looking out. Just above the windowsill a face was visible through the dirty glass; not a human face but a featureless mask with two dark slitted eyes, halfway up. It did not move.

'What is it?' Grace could hardly whisper the words.

'Look like your knight, man,' Salvo said. 'That's a helmet.'

Grace could admit to herself now that she had only dared to come up here again because she had been sure that in sunshine, with Salvo, everything would turn out to be normal, explicable, safe; like the shadow. She tugged at Salvo's arm. 'Let's go back. *Please*. Let's go back.'

Salvo recovered his poise. 'Calm down, Auntie. It's a helmet, that's all. Nobody in it.'

The helmet moved.

'Christ on a bike!' said Salvo.

Grace had always thought that you screamed when you were terrified, but she could not even squeak, could not move, waiting for the helmet to rise up as the shadow had done. But the helmet seemed to shift sideways, there was something white behind it, a hand, fluttering cloth. Grace shut her eyes and dug her fingers into Salvo's arm, trying to make him drag her away, but she felt him move forward instead and she opened her eyes to see him leaning over the fence.

'Your knight wearing an Oxfam T-shirt, man.'

On the other side of the glass a face had appeared alongside the helmet. The reason the helmet was level with the windowsill, Grace realized, was that it was standing on a workbench. The wearer of the Oxfam T-shirt was a girl of about her own age, staring out at them as blankly as the helmet had done.

'Sorry to say it, but I'm disappointed, man,' Salvo said. 'I *hate* rational explanations.'

'I never really thought it was a ghost,' Grace said.

'Of course,' Salvo was rambling on, 'that might be a little jumbie girl who'll knock us down dead with one glance of her fiery eye . . . I never live this down, man. Say nothing to no one.'

'Were you scared?' Grace said.

Salvo thought about it. 'Pleasantly startled,' he admitted at last.

Meanwhile the jumbie girl had retreated to the back of the room. Grace could just make out the blur of her white T-shirt through the dusty glass. She leaned over the fence and rapped on the window. The girl came forward again. Grace beckoned, 'Come out.'

The girl did not smile – *could* she be dead? – but she looked at them for a moment and then nodded, mouthing, 'Wait'.

There was something truly ghostlike about the way she faded into the darkness. Had she not been wearing white she would have vanished, but Grace saw daylight again as she opened a door at the back of the room, light that shone upon its other occupant. The huge hooked-hand shape was painted a metallic blue and between the thumb and finger were a pair of gleaming steel rollers. She thought of Frank's picture. She had to be right.

'Look, Salvo. Do you know what that is?'

'Oh, man,' Salvo breathed. 'Is that what you wanted me to see, Auntie?'

'Yes. Is it what I thought it was? I mean – *is* it?'

'Oh, you bet your sweet life, Auntie,' Salvo said. 'That's a wheeling machine. Now, how do we get our hands on it?'

Round the corner of the brick building came the jumbie girl.

'I didn't mean to frighten you,' she said. Her voice was very quiet and polite, as if she were making excuses to a teacher.

'I wasn't frightened,' Grace began. 'Not of you, it was the helmet.'

'It's not a helmet,' the girl said. 'It's a great helm. You're thinking of a bascinet. They came later.'

'A what?'

'The kind with the visor at the front that goes up and down. They went on using great helms in tournaments, but they're terribly heavy, no good in warfare. I can't even lift that one. We've got a bascinet indoors.'

Grace gaped at her. 'Have you got a knight as well?'

The girl kept looking nervously over her shoulder and before she could answer a voice close by called out, 'Dizzy!'

'Don't go away,' the girl said, and disappeared among the apple trees.

Salvo was gazing in at the window, his nose almost touching the glass.

'Is that a friendship you striking up there, man?'

'I don't know,' Grace said. 'She's a bit odd, isn't she?'

'You *got* to strike up a friendship,' Salvo said. 'Life was sad enough with no wheeling machine, but to see it and not to have it . . .'

Dizzy came back looking diminished, as though the sunlight were causing her to evaporate.

'I've got to go in, in a minute,' she said. 'For dinner. Do you live round here?'

'Not far,' Grace said, pointing vaguely.

'Could you come again? I could show you some more armour.'

'And the wheeling machine?' Grace said.

The girl smiled for the first time. 'You know what it is! Do you know how to work it?'

'He does,' Grace said, nodding towards Salvo who was now almost kissing the window.

'Yes, but you can come on your own, can't you?' Dizzy looked pitifully hopeful. 'You know, just to see me.'

'I'll try. Is this your own house?'

'Yes. You'd better come to the front next time. Mummy doesn't like me to be down here on my own. She's afraid strange people might come along the footpath. We're 19 Rectory Lane, next to the church but round the corner. Only, when you come, don't say we met down here. Say you've just started riding lessons and – no, she'd know that wasn't true. Where do you go to school?'

'Wing Farm,' Grace said.

'Where's that?'

'On Wing Farm Estate,' Grace said, beginning to suspect that Dizzy's mummy would not approve.

'Where those roofs are? I often wondered what was there. I've never been down there.'

'I never come up here,' Grace said. 'Well, not often. Only once.'

'I know,' Dizzy said, 'you go for a walk and we'll meet by accident. Can you come tomorrow?'

'Yes.' Salvo would help for sure now that he'd seen what was in it for him.

'I'll be in the churchyard.'

'When?'

'Half-past one, after lunch. If you come in the front way you go round the west end where the tower is, and you'll see our wall. There's a gap halfway down. I'll wait there. Then we can sort of meet by accident, even if there's someone watching.'

'Dizzy!' The voice came again.

'Is that your mum?' Grace said.

'No, Birgitta. She's the au pair. I'd better go. If I'm late Mummy gets cross with *her*.' Dizzy walked backwards, waving, over the grass, under the roses, among the lengthening shadows. 'Half-past one. Don't forget.' Only her T-shirt was visible now.

'Foot in the door, man,' Salvo said, when she was out of sight. 'We better wend our homeward way.'

'What do you mean, foot in the door?'

'Well, if you get friends with little Dizzy there, maybe me and Frank can get a crack at that wheeling machine. I wonder if they make armour on it.'

'Could you? Make armour on it, I mean.'

'Don't see why not,' Salvo said, taking a last lingering look at the wheeling machine. 'It only does what a panel-beater would do. And *some*one round here is making armour.'

'I'll have to get round Mum first,' Grace said. 'Even if I'm invited, it's still off the estate. Do you know how to get to Rectory Lane?'

''Course I do,' Salvo said. 'Remember the sinks and the tanks and the pipes. Even people with au pairs have S-bends.'

'What is an au pair?'

'Sort of maid,' Salvo said, 'only posher and not so well paid. Don't worry about that, Auntie. I'll stop by and give you a lift in me lunch break. Maybe bring you home, too. Take it a little at a time. Once your mum get used to you coming up here she won't worry so much, then she won't worry at all, maybe. Got to let you stretch your wings sometime.' He looked even more pleased with himself than usual. 'Wings; that's a good one, Auntie. I said we'd get you airborne again.'

'Y ou got your ticket of leave then, Auntie?' Salvo said, when Grace ran out to his blue Escort van at twenty-past one.

'My what?' She climbed in beside him and fastened the seat belt.

'You're allowed out on certain conditions.'

'Yes.'

'What's the conditions?'

'I've got to come home with you again.'

'Well, that's what we agreed, isn't it? I knock off at five, give or take. I'll pick you up.'

'We might not like each other,' Grace said,

thinking of Dizzy's pale serious face and cautious eyes. 'I might want to come home before that.'

'Well, I can cruise by around three, between jobs. But I should think you'd get on just fine. You found a soul-sister there, man.'

'What do you mean?'

'If you ask me, that's one more bored little girl with nothing to do. That big house, that huge garden, wall-to-wall au pairs, and what she do? Hang around all alone in a dirty shed.'

They were taking a different route in the van, past the end of the footpath and over the top of the hill. Here was another estate with blocks of flats, a business park, a hospital, a railway station. It occurred to Grace that she had seen more of London than she had of her own town.

Salvo turned off the main road past the hospital. Grace noticed that the streets were becoming leafier, the gardens larger. Some of the houses were old, really old, with timbering and thatch and fancy brick chimneys.

'Rectory Lane's the next on the left,' Salvo said. 'Look, you can see the church over those trees.'

'Suppose she isn't there,' Grace said. 'What shall I do?'

'I'll wait,' Salvo said. 'If you don't come back in a few minutes I'll go. If you do, I'll take you plumbing with me. That'll be an education.'

'And you *will* come by at three?'

'Three-ish,' Salvo said, turning the van into Rectory Lane. It was just as Grace had expected: the lawns, the tree-filled gardens, the houses with many windows and not a satellite dish in sight. 'Look, it's not like you to be worried, Auntie.'

'I don't want to get into more trouble.'

'OK, OK, I'll lurk till I'm sure you made contact. I'll watch,' Salvo said. 'I will not leave your side until I know all's well.'

They were parked by the church gate. A few metres farther on the road turned, and Grace saw a wide entry with white posts on either side. The number 19 was painted on both of them.

'Why do church gates have these little roofs on?' she said as they went through.

'They're called lich gates, man,' Salvo said. 'To put the coffin down under on the way to funerals. Now, don't you start imagining things,' he said, as Grace began looking round nervously at the silent graves. 'Remember, no spooks here, man. Only your Dizzy friend with her helmet.'

'Great helm,' Grace reminded him, wondering if Dizzy really would be her friend. In retrospect she seemed not quite real, less real than the knight. 'Do you like her?' she asked, as they skirted the war memorial and walked down a grassy path between yew trees.

'Hardly saw her,' Salvo said, 'but how come she called Dizzy I can't imagine. There she is, your poor little rich girl. Feel safe now?'

Dizzy was sitting on the wall of the churchyard at a place where the stones had fallen away. Leaning over her protectively was an angel with soaring wings.

'If things don't work out, be at the coffin cosy by three,' Salvo muttered, and loped away towards the lich gate. Dizzy, waving, slithered from the wall. Grace heard the van door slam and the engine rev.

'I was afraid you wouldn't come,' Dizzy said. 'I've been waiting and waiting.'

'Am I late?'

'No,' Dizzy said. 'I enjoy waiting.' She added strangely, 'Even if things don't happen you can enjoy waiting for them because you think they *will* happen.'

'Then you must have thought I was coming,' Grace said reasonably.

Dizzy gave her a small, uncertain smile. 'Yes, but I was still afraid you wouldn't. Come and meet the Blessed Damozel.'

'Is that the au pair?'

It was an honest mistake but Dizzy took it for a joke and giggled like a wind chime. 'No, that's Birgitta; she's a person. This is the Blessed Damozel.'

She was pointing at the angel. It was a blowsy-looking female with a tightly belted waist and a large bosom to which it clasped a bunch of rigid lilies in two clenched fists, as if they were some kind of Ninja weapon. It had a round fat face and piously upturned eyes with no pupils, and from under its robe poked two flat feet with enormous big toes. Seen close to it was greyish rather than white, but on its swelling stone cheek was one pale shiny patch.

'Her real name's Georgiana Ledbetter,' Dizzy said, indicating the inscription on the plinth upon which the angel was standing, 'but Gareth calls her the Blessed Damozel. It's out of a poem. She's our guardian angel. We always kiss her for good luck.'

That no doubt accounted for the smooth white patch on Georgiana Ledbetter's left cheek. Gareth; Grace thought of the Knights of the Round Table; *Sir* Gareth? She felt almost shy, and did not know what to say. She had never before met anyone quite like Dizzy, and she wished that Salvo had stayed a little longer. Salvo was seldom at a loss for words.

'What's *your* name?' Dizzy said suddenly. 'Isn't that odd? I don't even know what your name is.'

'Grace,' Grace said firmly, and was glad after all that Salvo had left before Dizzy had heard him calling her Auntie. 'Grace Thompson.'

'Blessed Damozel, meet Grace Thompson,' Dizzy said, bowing formally. 'I like doing introductions. Kiss her for luck,' she commanded.

Even without the plinth the angel was taller than the wheeling machine. Grace set one foot on the plinth and swung herself up by clasping Georgiana Ledbetter round the waist. The stone cheek was cool, in spite of the sunshine.

'Now,' Dizzy said, as she jumped down, 'if anyone asks, why are you here?'

'To see you,' Grace said.

'No, I meant what will you tell them? Haven't you got a cover story?' Grace wondered who Them was; the enemy? Was Dizzy playing spies? 'Remember, we're meeting by accident.'

Grace had overlooked this when she had told Mum that she had met someone who had invited

96

her over to play. She had not thought that they would actually be *playing*.

'I'll say I've come to look round the graves.'

'That'll sound funny. Say you're doing it for school.'

'All right.' Dizzy had started looking over her shoulder again. 'Does it matter?'

'Oh, yes. Mummy always wants to know where I've met people and I can't say I met you over the fence because I'm not allowed to go down there. I told you that.'

No, this was not precisely playing. 'My mum's always fussy about where I am too,' Grace said. But Mum was not fussy about who she played with. She remembered what Salvo had said, '. . . big house . . . huge garden . . . wall-to-wall au pairs . . .' She was beginning to get a feeling that she herself might turn out to be one of the things that Mummy was fussy about.

Dizzy looked over her shoulder. 'Let's go down among the trees.'

'Can we go and see the wheeling machine?'

Dizzy glanced at her watch. 'Not yet. Mummy's going out soon.' Grace was glad to follow her away from the gap in the wall, out of sight of the house, among the yews of the churchyard.

'Do you know how to work it?'

'The wheeling machine? Daddy and Gareth do; well, they know *how* but they aren't any good at it. When Gareth and Marian bought their farm it was in the kitchen and there wasn't room for it so they had it brought here, because Daddy said it was too valuable to part with. But Mummy wouldn't have it in the garage so it had to come down here. It took ages to move it, it weighs about a tonne, but Daddy said it was sure to come in useful, and then the armourer died.'

'Are they making armour on it?' Anything was possible here. If she hadn't misheard, Dizzy had said that someone kept the wheeling machine in the *kitchen*. 'Did they make the great helm?'

'No, John did that. The armourer. I'll show you where he's buried.'

She darted away among the graves. This end of the churchyard was overgrown and the grass was waist-high, with feathery seed heads. The trees made mottled shade and Dizzy flickered in and out of view between the headstones, renewing Grace's earlier suspicion that she was not really there. Sooner or later she knew, following Dizzy, she was going to have to ask outright, 'Am I imagining this or do you really make armour and dress up as knights?' But Dizzy did not yet know about the encounter through the telescope. Grace did not think that it was Dizzy she had seen that evening.

They had worked their way round to the north side of the church where there were no trees and fewer graves. The grass was clipped short and the stones were much smaller here, much newer. There were no angels. Dizzy stopped and knelt at a grave that was a simple bank of turf with a vase of asters balanced on top. At one end a small wooden cross had been thrust into the earth. Grace thought uneasily of vampires and stakes through the heart.

'Why hasn't it got a stone?'

'You can't put up a stone until the earth's settled,' Dizzy said matter-of-factly. 'That takes months. But the vicar said they could put up this cross to be going on with. See, here he is.'

'The vicar?' Grace looked round.

'*No*, the armourer. This is him, John James Sillinger.'

'It says St Leger,' Grace pointed out. 'Like the horse race.'

'Yes, but you say it Sillinger.'

'You don't the horse race.'

'It's different for people.' Dizzy traced the words painted on the cross. '*John James St Leger 1929–1994. Armourer and Soldier of Fortune with the Company of the White Horse. Invicta!* Isn't it a wonderful name for an armourer? And he had a brilliant death. He died at his bench and they found him with his head on a sandbag and his planishing hammer still *gripped* in his hand.' She tapped the cross again. 'That's us, soldiers of fortune. We're the Company of the White Horse.'

Grace wondered what was so brilliant about dropping dead with your head on a sandbag. Soldiers of fortune . . . that rang a bell. 'You dress up?'

'I don't, but Gareth does and Daddy used to. I pretend to be Gareth's squire, but I can't really join in because when the battle starts it's the rule that there mustn't be any non-combatants on the field. I expect I'll fight though when I'm grown up and no one can say I mustn't.'

'But who do you fight?'

Dizzy sat on John James St Leger's grave and hugged her knees happily. The hunted look had left her eyes. 'Oh, there's hundreds of people. Well, there's only eleven in the Company at the moment because they're a splinter group, they broke away from Sir Aylmer's Mercenaries, but they can always get a fight. Gareth likes to ride into battle because of Hendrickje – she's his horse –'

'His destrier?'

Dizzy looked delighted. 'You know! Well, she's not really a destrier; they were always stallions because they're fierce and like to fight.'

'That's why they were called destriers.' Grace felt that she was holding her own. 'Destroyers.'

'No, it wasn't that. The knight only rode his war horse into battle, he had a palfrey the rest of the time, and his squire led the war horse with his right hand, his dexter hand, that's Latin, *dexter*, destrier.'

Either Dizzy was wrong about this or Dad was. Grace had a feeling that it was Dad, and wondered whether to put him right.

'Who's Gareth?'

'My uncle.'

'And he rides a horse – wearing armour?'

'That's it. He leads the Company. He's a knight.'

'I think I've seen him,' said Grace.

They made their way down the garden, between the rose bushes, under the apple trees.

'I thought you weren't meant to come down here,' Grace said.

Dizzy's eyes flicked over her shoulder and down at her watch in a nervous tic. 'Only on my own. I'm not on my own now, am I?'

Grace was all the time waiting for that sharp voice she had heard yesterday, calling for Dizzy, and then she would have to explain herself; but they reached the chestnut palings unchallenged.

'Now,' Dizzy said, 'show me exactly where you were.'

Grace pointed. 'See over the trees, those long roofs? That's the bus depot. Now, see those allotments on the other side, and that row of houses? See the house on the end with the window in the roof? That's where I was.'

'We haven't got a telescope,' Dizzy said. 'But Daddy has binoculars. I wonder if I could see right in. We could wave to each other.'

'It's not my house, and I don't suppose I'll ever be up there again. You can only see the roof of mine. That's our chimney, on the end,' Grace said.

'And you looked through the telescope just as Gareth came out of the workshop. And it was the first time you'd ever been up there. I think that's Fate,' Dizzy said impressively. 'If you hadn't seen him, you'd never have come up here looking and I'd never have met you. Do you realize, if you'd been one minute earlier or one minute later you wouldn't have seen him? He was just going up to the house to get his lance.'

'Was he going to fight?'

'No, we were taking photographs. Anyway, he doesn't fight on horseback because of Hendrickje not being trained. But he leads the Company of the White Horse when they take the field, and sometimes he fights on foot, or lays an ambush. The Company hasn't been going very long, but soon they'll issue challenges and have proper battles with other companies, and Gareth can be a real knight and go to tournaments. He and Daddy thought they might try to make armour for Hendrickje on the wheeling machine.'

Armour for a horse? 'Can we go and look at it now?'

'The wheeling machine? All right.' Dizzy led the way round to the side of the brick building. 'You see, now John James St Leger's dead, the Company haven't got anybody to make their armour. He didn't make it just for them, but he belonged; he followed the White Horse. Most of the Company have got enough armour because they're foot soldiers and don't need much, but new members will need arming, and Gareth does want to be a real knight.'

Dizzy might be slow to get going, but there was no stopping her once she was in top gear. Grace was gradually taking in the fact that what she was describing was a group of *adults*.

Dizzy opened a blistered, brown-painted door. To the left rose a rickety flight of wooden stairs with, Grace noticed, a light fitted to the wall where they turned, halfway up. To the right was the workshop with its dirty window facing the footpath, and the wheeling machine.

Now that she was close up to it Grace could hardly believe how big it was. Her eyes were below the level of the rollers and high above those it curved upward to the ceiling, over and down again. The base was bolted to the concrete floor and stacked against it were sheets of metal, some cut about and twisted, rather like Frank's aborted mudguard in the garage at home. Evidently someone had been practising. Dizzy wrapped an arm around the wheeling machine and perched on the base. Grace looked for the great helm and saw that it had been draped in a cloth.

'We were afraid someone would steal it,' Dizzy said, seeing where she was looking. 'That's what I was doing last night, covering it up. Gareth's coming back for it. He only brought it along for the photographs.'

'Can I look?' Grace put out her hand to move the cloth but before she could touch it the door creaked open and someone entered. Could this be Birgitta?

'Mummy!' Dizzy said guiltily, and slid off the wheeling machine. 'I thought you'd gone out.'

'Obviously. How many times have I told you to stay away from here?' the woman said, peering. 'Who is that with you?'

'This is Grace,' Dizzy said. 'Grace, this is my mother. We met in the churchyard –'

'What were you doing in the churchyard?' Grace's mother said. She did not sound remotely friendly, or remotely motherly, come to that. She did not look like a mother, more like somebody on breakfast television who had got up at 4 a.m. to put her face on.

'Oh, I was just sitting on the wall and I saw

103

Grace in the churchyard and we started talking and she knows all about wheeling machines –' Dizzy gabbled desperately.

'No, what were *you* doing in the churchyard?' Mummy was speaking to Grace. What a good thing Dizzy had insisted on a cover story – and no wonder she had.

'Um . . . just finding out something for school,' Grace said. 'Just looking at names on graves and that, for a topic.'

'Which school would that be?'

'Wing Farm Primary.'

'On the estate?' She might have said 'Beyond the Pale?' for that was clearly what she meant.

'Yes.'

'Rather a long way from home, aren't you?'

'I got a lift. I'm being collected. At three.' She had almost said five, but decided to play safe. 'Ish.'

Mummy looked at her watch. 'Have you finished your investigations?'

'My what?'

'In the graveyard, for your *topic*.'

'Nearly. Yes.'

'Oh, she can stay. Can't she stay? She doesn't *have* to go at three,' Dizzy pleaded, but Grace saw a hopeless look on her face. This must have happened before, Dizzy bringing home the Wrong Sort of Friend. But Mummy knew how to deal with it.

Mummy softened, slightly. 'Well, I expect there is just time for you both to have some orange juice. Come along.'

She stood back and they filed out past her.

Grace heard a key turning in the lock behind them.

The kitchen was like one of the displays at B&Q, the kind you knew no one used. This one did not look as if it had ever been used. Nothing stood on the long pine table except for a bowl of roses. There were no coffee mugs draining by the sink; no teatowels or discloths or old pot-scourers lying about; nobody's muddy boots on the mat; no mat even, just spotless brown tiles. No smell of cooking hung about it and the hob, set in the work surface, looked so clean it might just have been installed. Under the work surfaces was nothing but cupboards and drawers of pale polished wood. Where was the washing machine, the fridge?

Grace had thought that they would at least be left alone to fetch their own orange juice, which was why she had been looking for the fridge, but Dizzy, who had gone very quiet again, stood by the table until her mother came in and shut the door.

She went over to the worktop beside the oven and opened a cupboard. The fridge was behind it, concealed by the panelling. Surely the washing machine was not panelled too? Mummy looked into the fridge, appeared displeased, straightened up and called, 'Birgitta!'

'I think she's in the utility room,' Dizzy whispered. 'Ironing. She'll have her Walkman on.'

Mummy glided across the tiles and opened a door. On the far side was a room lined with all the things that most people had to cram into their kitchens and garages, or do without: a washing machine, a tumble drier, a chest freezer and an upright freezer. In the middle were an ironing board and a table stacked with piles of clothes. Between them stood a girl with a personal stereo round her waist, ironing a shirt with quick erratic stabs, keeping time to a rhythm that only she could hear.

Seeing the door open she whipped out the earphones.

'Yes, Mrs Morley?'

'There is no orange juice, Birgitta,' Mrs Morley said, speaking very distinctly, as if to a lip-reader. 'Why is there no orange juice? I asked you to make some.'

'We have not oranges,' Birgitta said cheerfully.

'Why didn't you tell me? Why didn't you get some when you went shopping?'

'I go shopping before I know there are not oranges,' Birgitta said.

'You ought to have checked. I asked you to tell me what we needed when I made the list.'

'While you are making the list there are oranges. While I come back from the shop there are not oranges.' Birgitta set the iron aside, shook out the shirt and hung it from the drying rack above her head. When she looked round she seemed to have been visited by inspiration. 'I think the oranges are being eaten.'

Mrs Morley turned to Dizzy. 'Have you eaten the oranges?'

'No, Mummy,' Dizzy said. 'Really, Mummy, I didn't, well, I had one, I only had one.'

'You will just have to make do with milk. I do

wish you children would not take things without asking.' This complaint seemed to include Grace, who was the only other child present. Mrs Morley closed the door of the utility room without another glance at Birgitta, so she did not see, as Grace saw, Birgitta bent double over the ironing board, trying not to laugh out loud. Grace could understand what she was laughing at but she did not think it was funny. Left to get on with it at home they would have found themselves something to drink and gone out again, in the time it had taken Mummy to investigate The Strange Affair of the Disappearing Oranges.

She gave them instead a glass of milk each, poured by her own hand from a jug in the fridge. Then she stood silently by while they drank it. Grace disliked drinking milk on its own but did not have the nerve to say so. Dizzy's mother reminded her of a creature in a book she had once read, that turned everything to ice as it went past.

Mrs Morley broke the silence.

'Who is coming to collect you, Grace?'

'A friend. I said I'd wait at that coffin place by the church.'

'The lich gate?'

'Yeah, that's right.' This must be what Frank called getting the bum's rush.

'Well, you had better not wait alone. Dizzy may stay with you – no, not that way,' she said, as Dizzy made for the back door. 'Go round through the front garden, and come straight back, Dizzy, as soon as Grace has got her lift. Goodbye, Grace. It was so nice meeting you.'

Grace followed Dizzy out of the kitchen, wondering how she could face telling Salvo that she had not only found the wheeling machine, but lost it again.

Chapter Eight

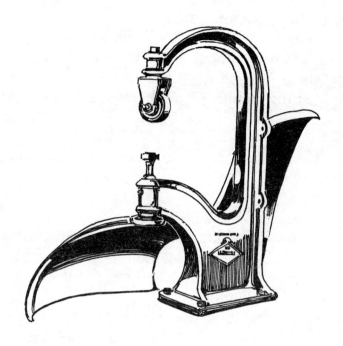

Dizzy led the way through a hall as big as Grace's bedroom, with a floor of highly polished wood blocks. There must be half a dozen doors at least leading out of that hall, Grace calculated as they went by. The front door was a huge panelled thing with stained glass pictures in it. Dizzy opened it wordlessly, ushered Grace through and closed it carefully behind them. Grace wanted to say, 'Is your mother always like that?' but presumably she was and Dizzy was used to it. Instead she said, 'Perhaps you can come down mine, some time?'

'Yes. Maybe,' Dizzy said, falsely cheerful.

'I can always come up the churchyard again. We can meet by your Bloody Amazon.'

Dizzy laughed at last. 'Blessed Damozel. It's a good thing Mummy didn't hear you call her that.'

Grace privately agreed.

There was nothing in the Morleys' front garden except gravel and a hostile-looking monkey puzzle tree in the middle. Grace followed Dizzy between the white-painted posts, and they walked to the lich gate.

'They're late,' Dizzy said, looking at the church clock.

'Who?'

'Your lift.'

'He only said three-ish,' Grace said. It was two minutes past. She was afraid that Salvo might have come and gone, thinking that all was well. 'He's between jobs.'

'What jobs? What does he do?'

'He's a plumber,' Grace said. 'That was him with me last night; he's the one who knows how to work the wheeling machine. He's my brother's friend. They've got this very old coal lorry and they're renovating it.'

'What for? Are they going to sell coal?'

'They're going to show it at the steam rally at Arling in the Historic Commercial Vehicle class, and they've spent three years making it new again. Really, it was an old wreck when they got it and now it looks like it's just been built. Only they haven't got any mudguards for it. That's why they need a wheeling machine – that's what it's for, making curves in metal.' Grace knew now that it didn't matter how many hints she dropped to Dizzy, Dizzy had no influence whatsoever. 'My dad runs the steam rally.'

'Runs it?' Dizzy was impressed. 'Is that his job?'

'No, he doesn't get paid. There's a whole bunch of them and he's Hon. Sec.' Grace saw the blue van coming round the corner. 'Here's Salvo. My lift.'

'Salvo? Is that his real name?'

'Claude Salvatore. Is Dizzy your real name?'

'It's Isabelle. Daddy used to call me Dizzabella.' Grace was surprised that Mummy had allowed that.

Salvo stopped the van and climbed out. Seeing them together he looked at his watch and raised his eyebrows.

'So soon, Auntie?'

'Auntie!' Dizzy exploded.

'Dizzy's got to go, so I thought I'd better come home now,' Grace said hastily. Dizzy did not contradict.

'I'll see you sometime,' she said as Grace and Salvo got into the van.

'I'll come to the churchyard,' Grace said. 'I'll wait by the Bloody Amazon.' She knew perfectly well now that it was the Blessed Damozel, but she wanted to see Dizzy laugh again. Dizzy just smiled and stood by the lich gate, waving forlornly as they drove away.

'Did you have a mighty falling-out?' Salvo said. 'You seemed to be getting on OK when I blew in.'

'She goes on a bit,' Grace admitted, 'but she's

all right. She's nice. Oh, Salvo, it wasn't her. Her mother!'

'Often a problem,' Salvo said wisely, 'mothers.'

'She was horrible. I mean horribly polite. She wouldn't let me stay. It was the estate, when she knew I lived on the estate. I could almost see her sniffing to see if I smelt bad.'

'Good thing she didn't see *me*,' Salvo remarked. 'One look at me dreads and she'd be screaming the Yardies are here. And yet, if her toilet backed up, she'd be begging me down the phone, offering untold riches.'

'I'm sorry about the wheeling machine,' Grace said. 'Dizzy took me to see it. Oh, Salvo, it's beautiful, and they don't know how to use it. I mean, they aren't even proper knights yet. They're only *trying* to make armour on it, I saw the bits, they don't know what they're doing. They're trying to make armour for a horse.'

'Dizzy's mother's making armour for a horse?'

'No, her dad and her uncle; and there was this dead man in the churchyard, named after a horse race.'

'Derby?' Salvo said, vaguely. 'Cheltenham Gold Cup? OK if I drop you at the end of Wing Farm Drive, Auntie? I got to get out to Springfield next.'

'It's OK with me. I don't suppose Mum will mind.' Whatever her faults, not for the world would Grace have swapped her mother for Dizzy's.

She got out of the van. 'I'm sorry about the wheeling machine, Salvo,' she said again.

'Don't worry about it,' Salvo said. 'Love will find a way and, man, do I *love* that wheeling machine.'

Grace was worried later that she had not made it clear enough to Salvo, the incurable optimist, that he had no hope of getting at the wheeling machine; that Mrs Morley had made it coldly clear, without actually saying so, that she did not expect to see Grace at the house again, or in the garden, and certainly not in the workshop.

Only a week ago none of this had even begun to happen. She had not known about Dizzy and her guardian angel, the knight, the wheeling machine up there on the hillside. She had scarcely known the hillside existed. Now it was Friday evening again and she was back where she'd started; Mum and Lynette were upstairs getting ready for the Maid of Kent, taking turns in the bathroom with Helen who was going to try out a new boyfriend at the cinema. Frank was in the garage waiting for Salvo to pick him up on their way to the Fox and Hounds. Dad was up at Arling to look after arrangements for the rally, and until he came back Grace was just where she had been before, facing another evening alone at home. Last week she had thought she hadn't minded. Now she knew that she minded very much.

If only they did not live in the Close; if they did not live at the end of the Close. On the other roads of the estate people passed each other's houses, passed people waving from windows or sitting on doorsteps or leaning over gates, ran into groups of friends at the shops. No matter how long she sat on her doorstep or leaned from the window, no one ever walked along the Close because it led nowhere. The only people who came up this far were the ones who lived here, the Milners and the Thompsons.

Grace, lolling over the gate, looked up at the skylight. There, predictably, was Sarah Carr, waiting for a glimpse of Frank. The scaffolding was gone now, so she had an uninterrupted view. Probably Steffi was at the back, leaning out of her window, staring at the corner house where her boyfriend lived. Later they would do what they always did. Grace saw them every evening stroll down the Close and turn right at the bottom. She could guess what happened after that: they would cross the Sittingbourne Road, walk up Barrack Hill and stake out the corner house in Denmark Road. They were old enough to go where they liked, when they liked, and anyway, they had each other for company and reinforcements.

A green sports car was coming up the Close; it was an Austin-Healey 3000 with the top down, and moving very slowly. The driver was looking from side to side, as if he were searching for a particular house. Grace watched the car crawl to the end of the Close and stop as the driver realized that it was a dead end and did not go round the corner. He went on peering, no doubt wondering if there would be room to turn, particularly at the Thompsons' drive where the Fordson left about two metres clear. Then he saw Grace.

He switched off the engine and climbed out.

Grace, aware that Sarah was now almost falling out of the skylight, noticed that he was young and tall, with floppy fair hair that gleamed whitely against his tanned face. He came up to the gate.

'You couldn't possibly be Grace Thompson, could you?' he asked, so courteously that Grace could have sworn he was bowing. She hoped Sarah could hear. He had actually come looking for *her*. She also hoped that Mum was still in the bathroom. If she looked out of her bedroom window and saw Grace talking to a strange man over the gate she would be down there with them, faster than light.

'Yes, that's me,' Grace said.

'And this is the house exactly behind the house with the new window in the roof?'

'Yes.'

'Can you tell me where I can find Mr Salvatore, please?'

'Salvo?' Grace said. 'You're not the police, are you?'

'Why, is he on the run?' the young man said.

'Oh, no.' Grace knew that her suspicions were the result of seeing too many cop shows on television. 'I just wondered why you were looking for him here.'

'I don't know where he lives,' the stranger said, 'but I was reliably informed that I could find him by inquiring at the house behind the house with the window in the roof. I was shown it through binoculars and worked out where it must be on the map. I'm Gareth Morley,' he said, 'Dizzy's uncle.'

'You're the knight!'

'I am, yes. I believe we've met before, if only at a distance.'

'I saw you through a telescope,' Grace said. 'If I hadn't seen you I wouldn't have met Dizzy.'

'If you hadn't met Dizzy I wouldn't be here. Do you have Mr Salvatore's address?'

'You can call him Salvo,' Grace said. 'Everybody does, except his girlfriend. He lives down the town, in the Carlton Court flats, but he'll be here soon. Do you want to wait?'

'If I may.' He was behaving just as she thought a knight ought to behave, and treating her like a grown-up, speaking to her as nobody else did, except, now that she came to think about it, Salvo, although he did it differently.

'You're not on your own, are you?' Gareth Morley said, as she opened the gate for him. 'Perhaps I'd better wait out here.'

'Oh, it's all right,' Grace said, but grateful for his concern. 'Everybody's in.' She wondered how she was going to explain him to everybody, and stopped on her way to the side gate. 'Why do you want to see Salvo?'

He might very well have said 'Mind your own business,' but he just smiled. 'Dizzy says you told her he knows how to operate a wheeling machine. We thought he might give us a demonstration, or even a few lessons.'

'Oh, he would, he'd love to,' Grace cried, omitting to add that this was just what Salvo had been hoping for.

116

'Dizzy also said that if he came, you might come with him.'

Grace, acknowledging that even if Dizzy had no influence, she was cunning, was about to ask bluntly what Mummy thought of this bright idea, when Frank ambled out of the garage.

'Did I hear a Big Healey?' Frank said.

'This is my brother,' Grace said. 'He knows about wheeling machines too. Frank, this is my friend's uncle. He's got a wheeling machine.'

'Evening, Uncle,' Frank said, holding out a hand larded with axle grease. Gareth shook it without flinching. 'That your car, man?'

'Yes.'

'What year?'

'1960.'

'Mark II?'

'No, an original. Want to look?'

'Sure. Then you come and see our Fordson. 1947 7V, that's the back of it, there. So you're the guy with the wheeling machine. The rest of it was no problem. Hard work, man, but no problem. But now we've nearly finished and we've got stuck over the mudguards —'

They had forgotten about her. In thirty seconds flat one fanatic had met another and now she might just as well have been on a different planet. Gareth, the knight in shining armour, driver of an Austin-Healey and, apparently, brother-in-law of Mummy, was out there in the Close with Frank; *Frank*. When he first emerged from the garage she had been ready to pretend that he was just someone who happened to be passing, nothing to do with her.

She leaned over the gate again, watching the two of them fossicking about beneath the bonnet of the Austin-Healey. Next thing, Frank would have him down in the inspection pit under the Fordson, sump oil dripping in his golden hair. Without looking directly she observed that Sarah was no longer at the skylight. With Steffi she had come downstairs and the pair of them were being tremendously busy doing nothing at all in the Milners' front garden.

Up the road came Salvo in his Friday-evening-out gear: clean blue jeans, white collarless shirt and a gold brocade waistcoat with a crimson back. In his right ear gleamed one perfect amber teardrop, the colour of marmalade. He saw Grace and raised a hand in salute. Then he saw the Austin-Healey.

'Frank, man, you nicked yourself some wheels. Why you not ready? It's nearly seven.'

'Salvo.' Grace beckoned him over. 'Remember Dizzy?'

'Vaguely,' Salvo said. 'In the mists of time she float, indistinctly.'

Gareth's head appeared from under the bonnet.

'Salvo, this is her uncle. He's come about the wheeling machine.'

'You go on ahead,' Mum said to Lynette. 'I want to get this sorted out. Now, Frank, you're going up to St Dunstan's with Salvo and you want to take Auntie. You *want* to take Auntie?'

'To be frank,' said Frank, 'Auntie's part of the deal. We're going up to see Auntie's friend's uncle

118

– that's him out there. Auntie wants to see her friend. We're going in his car.'

'That's a two-seater,' Mum said, looking out of the window by the front door. 'You're not all piling into that.'

'He drives ever so slowly,' Grace said. 'I've seen him.' Mum could not forbid Frank to pile into the Austin-Healey, Frank was old enough to vote, but she could forbid Grace. Surely she was not going to be made to stay at home while the rest sailed off without her.

'It's a 2 + 2,' Frank said. 'Very rare on a Big Healey. I was telling him he ought to enter it at Arling, in the Classic Cars.'

'I don't care how rare it is. Is it safe? And how's she getting home again?'

'Someone'll bring her,' Salvo said. 'We'll walk back with her, if you like.'

'Just so long as she isn't left to come back alone. And I want her back here by nine-thirty, understood?'

'Trust me, Jacquie,' Salvo said, and pressed his thumb and forefinger together, like the wheeling machine.

Grace was almost disappointed to find Gareth observing the speed limit all the way, but he swept into the drive of 19 Rectory Lane in an extravagant curve and braked on a satisfying spray of gravel. Mrs Morley was not the sort of person who lurked behind lace curtains, spying on the neighbours, Grace was sure, but she wondered if she might not be watching from one of her many rooms, and what she would say when she saw them all climbing out of the car along with the sections of rolled sheet steel that Salvo had brought with him. In the boot was stowed the frail remains of the Fordson's front off-side mudguard.

'Might as well go straight down to the workshop,' Gareth said, leading the way round the side of the house. Grace ran after him.

'Where's Dizzy?'

'Down at the workshop.'

'But her mum —'

'Is at a bridge evening,' Gareth said. 'Dizzy's with her father, clearing the place up. It's going to be a full house tonight.'

Dizzy was, in fact, halfway up the garden, having heard the car. She flung herself at Grace.

'Isn't it brilliant? You can join the Company too. You can be the armourer's assistant and come up here whenever you like. Hullo, Salvo. Can I call you Salvo? Who's that?'

'It's my brother Frank,' Grace said. Dizzy was tranformed from the nervous twitchy creature who had met Grace that afternoon, transformed from the sad and solitary figure who had waved good-bye to her only four hours ago.

'Your brother,' Dizzy said, wistful again. There seemed to be no half-measures with Dizzy. 'I wish I had a brother or something.'

'Have Frank, he's something,' Grace said. 'I've got two brothers and three sisters.'

'I haven't got anyone,' Dizzy said. 'Just an uncle. Why did Salvo call you Auntie this afternoon?'

Frank and Salvo had gone into the workshop with Gareth. Grace waited outside for a moment.

'It's a joke,' she said. 'I'm the youngest, see? Everyone else is grown up. My sister Lynette, she's *thirty*. She already had a baby when I was born. Now I've got two nieces and three nephews and one of them's older than me. I was born an aunt.' She was afraid Dizzy would laugh, but she looked envious. 'And there's another one due soon, but I don't know whether it'll be a niece or a nephew.'

'Can I call you Auntie?' Dizzy said, as if this would make her one of the family.

Grace felt her heart sink. 'Everyone calls me Auntie,' she said. 'Even at school. Can't you call me Grace?'

'All right,' Dizzy said. 'And I'll tell everyone else you're Grace. My great-grandmother was called Grace,' she added, which made Grace feel even more out of date than Auntie did.

They went into the workshop, with difficulty, because Frank and Salvo and Gareth were huddled round the wheeling machine, cooing over it like Mum when a new baby came along. Like Mum, Salvo was offering advice; 'You want to keep those rollers under wraps, man,' and like the mother of a new baby, someone was saying defensively, 'Well, we do usually . . .'

Grace looked among the crush for the speaker. He was over by the window, a thin, fair man, rather like Gareth but older, or more worn out. Dizzy pulled Grace towards him.

'Daddy, this is my friend Grace.'

Grace had secretly wondered what Mummy's husband would be like, but Dizzy's father was wearing overalls and work boots, 8-hole DMs, Grace noted with approval. He did not pretend to smile; he grinned, and Grace saw how like him to look at Dizzy was. Were they both scared of Mummy?

She expected him to say something, but he just nodded and gently motioned to them to stand by him out of the way. When she caught his eye he smiled at her, but still said nothing. Perhaps he was shy. She had never thought that a grown man could be shy. Dizzy climbed up on to the bench and Grace sat beside her.

'Right,' Gareth said, 'Salvo will now give us a demonstration of how to operate a wheeling machine.'

'He's going to make a mudguard,' Dizzy chipped in.

'Not tonight, man,' Salvo said. 'That would take hours, and we don't have hours. No, there's enough of the front off-side to weld patches on. I'm going to make a patch. Will try to.' He picked up one of his steel cut-outs, inserted it between the rollers and adjusted the pressure. Then he held aloft the dead mudguard. 'This is where the patch will go. What I got to do is find the centre of curvature on here and form the same contour on the patch. Now, it won't happen all at once, but you'll see that as I run it between the rollers it will begin to curve. I'm not bending it, that would produce a curve in just one direction. The wheeling machine makes a three-dimensional curve. Watch.'

Grace had never seen Salvo so serious even though he was standing before them in the light of the evening sun in a fancy waistcoat, with an amber stud in one ear. He sounded like someone explaining things on *Tomorrow's World*, only this was yesterday's world.

Gripping the metal firmly by the sides Salvo began to roll it backwards and forwards through the wheeling machine, and at the same time he too began to rock backwards and forwards.

'Look at me,' Salvo said, unnecessarily, for they were all gazing at him. 'Only the joints of me knees and ankles moving; the rest of me's as steady as the machine. Any move *I* make goes into the metal; we don't want that.' Grace kept her eyes fixed on the piece of steel. You could not see anything happening but little by little the metal was changing shape, mysteriously curving.

'Come on Frank, take the other end, get the feel of it, man.' Frank stepped forward like someone called out of the audience to assist a magician, and laid hold of the curving steel. For an instant he and Salvo reminded Grace of Mum and Helen, folding sheets, then Frank too began to rock, picking up Salvo's momentum, until they seemed to be partners in a silent dance, and all the while the steel curved over and round as they passed it through the rollers. On the wall behind them their shadows swayed back and forth in perfect time.

'It's like magic, isn't it?' Dizzy said, in her ear. 'I mean, they're not doing anything, and the machine's not doing anything, it's just happening.'

Chapter Nine

Mum was not best pleased when she came home at a quarter to twelve and found Grace in the garage watching Frank and Salvo cutting out sheet steel.

'I thought I could trust you,' she said to Salvo, ignoring Frank. There was no question of trusting Frank. 'Bed,' she said to Grace.

'We got her home as promised,' Salvo said, neglecting to add that it had been nearer to eleven than nine-thirty, 'but it was an evening of wonders, man, and all down to Auntie. We couldn't leave her out.'

Don't mention the telescope, Grace prayed silently.

'We may have found us a new career, man. Armourers.'

'We're joining the Company, man,' Frank said.

'What as, managing director? Tell me another; Where's your dad?'

'He was in bed when we got in,' Frank said.

'At half-past nine?'

'Shall I make some coffee?' Grace said hurriedly, before an interrogation could start.

'At this time of night? Cocoa. And then you can get yourself off upstairs.'

They sat round the table in the kitchen. 'This beats karaoke any night,' Salvo said.

'Who *are* these people?' Mum demanded. Grace thought that probably Mrs Morley was asking precisely the same question. She had returned just as they were leaving.

'Bill Morley's in oil,' Frank said.

'In oil? What is he, a sardine?'

'Gareth has a farm.'

'That's why he's got a horse,' Grace said.

'You don't have to be a farmer to have a horse. I thought I told you to get to bed.'

'Dizzy has riding lessons.'

'And what does her mother do?'

Salvo spluttered into his cocoa. 'I wish Birgitta was here,' he said. 'I was talking to her. She'd tell you.'

Salvo had been talking to Birgitta for most of the evening, when he wasn't talking about ductility and tensile strengths with Gareth and Dizzy's father.

'She told me, "I am in the utilery'oom –"'

'In the what?'

'Utility room, that what she calls it. "I am in the utilery'oom and I am ironing and I am emptying the washing machine and I am also coming into the kitchen to make the coffee and Mrs Morley is sitting with her friend and she is saying, "It is a full-time job running a house this size." That Birgitta, she lives in the present,' Salvo said fondly.

'She made us all drinks,' said Frank, 'and then she was going out again, and Bill said –'

'Oh, it's Bill already, is it?'

'What d'you expect us to call him; sir? He says, "Aren't you staying?" and she says, "Am I being allowed?" and he says, "Allowed? You're being invited," so she stayed. She's a cracker,' Frank said.

'Mmmm,' Salvo said thoughtfully.

'I bet Old Mother Morley keeps her in the utilery'oom out of the way, like Cinderella.'

'That is one ugly sister,' Salvo agreed.

Grace had been wondering what Mrs Morley had said when she and the boys had left. They had all been sitting, like this, in the kitchen, round the big pine table which Gareth and Salvo had covered with sheets of paper and sketches and books about armour, once the property of the late John James St Leger; but there were worse things than these on display. Gareth had rushed out and bought burgers and samosas and Coke, French fries and cartons of squelching coleslaw, and the remains of this forbidden food were scattered among the books and papers. Dizzy had confided

127

to Grace that she was never allowed any of it, ever, and she was the first to jump guiltily when a car door slammed outside. The others had been making too much racket to notice – they were not drinking Coca-Cola – but Dizzy had been getting edgier as the evening wore on. When the car door slammed she had leapt up, crying, 'I'll ring you tomorrow,' to Grace, and belted upstairs.

'Time for a quick sharp exit,' Gareth had muttered and they had basely fled too, leaving Bill and Birgitta to face Mummy; racing round the side of the house to the Austin-Healey just as she was opening the front door. She had stood frozen upon the step with her mouth half open, watching them scramble into the car while Gareth shouted, 'Hullo, Maggie, goodbye!' and started reversing before Salvo could get the door shut. It was like a scene on telly and Grace could hardly believe that she had been a part of it instead of sitting in front of the set, watching and laughing.

'This Gareth, had he been drinking?' Mum pounced, determined to find something wrong. 'With Grace in the car?'

'No, man, not even a beer. He's a good bloke, is Gareth,' Salvo said. 'I'm going out to look at his septic tank tomorrow.'

'Yes,' Mum said, cuttingly. 'I can see you have a lot in common. And that reminds me, there's a note from Ron by the phone says Venetia rang up three times this evening.'

*

'Who was that round yours yesterday?' Steffi demanded, waylaying Grace on her way back from the shop next morning.

'A friend of ours,' Grace said, stepping round her.

'What do you mean, *ours*? He's not *your* friend.'

'My friend's uncle,' Grace said. 'Same thing.'

'Who is he?' Now Steffi was walking alongside her. 'Oh, go on, Auntie, don't be a pig. Who is he?'

Grace thought of all the times she had hoped that one day she and Steffi could walk together and talk about interesting things, and of all the times Steffi had sent her packing; of all the snubby things that Steffi had said: 'Get lost, *little girl* . . . Get back to the infants . . . What's 'oo grizzling about, den? Has 'oo lost 'oo's dummy?'

But then, if it hadn't been for Steffi, Grace would never have been up in the loft with the telescope. She decided to be generous.

'I told you, he's my friend Dizzy's uncle. He's got a horse called Hendrickje and Dizzy and me are going out to see her soon.'

'Dizzy! What sort of a name do you call that?'

The generous impulse withered.

'It's short for Isabelle, like Steffi's *supposed* to be short for Stephanie. What sort of a name do you call *that*?'

'If he can afford a horse it's a pity he can't afford a decent car instead of that clapped-out old heap he was in last night.'

'It's not clapped out. It goes like a bomb and it's a very rare model. It's valuable.'

'Like the coal lorry. Must be awful never having anything new.' Steffi wisely abandoned the subject of Gareth and reverted to being personal, as usual.

They had reached the top of the Close. 'At least *my* friends come and see me,' Grace said. 'I don't have to hang around outside their houses and spy on them through telescopes. Sorry, can't stop. I'm expecting a phonecall.'

She dodged up the drive and round the back of the Fordson before Steffi could lay hold on her and administer one of her jabs. Dizzy would not be calling just yet, she knew, because she had her riding lesson on Saturday, but she had promised to ring as soon as she got back. And anyway, it could not be long before they all went up to St Dunstan's again, to make mudguards, or armour.

She skipped through the kitchen, leaving the shopping on the table. Helen had left for work, Mum was over at Gavin's again. Once she had sorted the mail there would be nothing to do except wait for Dizzy's call. Perhaps she might tidy her half of the bedroom, which was surely the smallest half in the world, barely a third, in case Dizzy ever escaped to visit her.

There was no mail on the mat. Grace went to the door to see if anything had caught in the letter flap. The delivery had been late today, but she knew that the postman had been round because he had passed them on his way down the Close while she was talking to Steffi; surely they must have got something.

She went into the living room where Dad was

sitting in his office. In front of him, on the desk, was a stack of letters, newly opened. She saw the envelopes in the waste bin.

'That's my job,' she said.

'Not any more,' Dad said. She looked at him. He was angry, really angry, not just cross.

'Why not? What have I done? Is it because I was up late last night? I won't do it again –'

'It's got nothing to do with last night. It's got everything to do with last week. What do you call this?'

For a moment Grace thought it must be a blackmailing letter about the telescope, but then she saw the letterhead. It looked familiar. *Motomaniax*; the stunt team who were performing at the rally.

She stared at it. It seemed to her that she had seen it before, quite recently.

'Do you know where I found it?'

'No.'

'On top of the bookcase, next to the maps. If I hadn't been looking for something, I'd never have noticed it. And how did it get up there?'

'I don't know. It wasn't me.'

'Yes it was!' Dad smacked his hand on the table. 'Look at the date, 22 July. That's Friday before last. You left this up there, didn't you, while you were looking at the maps last week?'

She remembered now; the last letter, the urgent letter, that she had meant to put somewhere prominent for Dad to find at once. She must still have been holding it when she climbed up to the map shelf, and as she remembered, she saw her right hand reaching out to rest the envelope on top of a box file.

'I thought I'd told you never to touch the maps.'

'I'm sorry, Dad. It wasn't important, was it?' The word URGENT hung in fiery letters before her eyes.

'Was it important? Yes, as it happens, it was very important. It was bad enough then, it's even worse now. It's been up there a whole week. A whole week when I could have been doing something about it. It's from Motomaniax. You know who they are?'

'Yes.'

'You know what they were going to do?'

Were? 'They're putting on a show at the rally.'

'No they aren't,' Dad said. 'This letter says they are very sorry but three of the members were involved in an accident at an event in Sunderland and they have had to cancel all engagements for the rest of the summer. You know what cancelled means?'

'They're not coming.'

'No, they're not coming. And this cheque, which is stapled to the letter and which you cheerfully left lying around for a week, is for £300. It's the returned deposit on their booking fee. Now that deposit should be recycled into booking someone else. I've got less than two weeks left. Three would have been bad enough; two's almost impossible. This is the height of the season, everbody's already booked up. And it's too late to stop the printers.'

'I'm sorry,' Grace said again. There was nothing

else to say. She had been trusted to do one thing and she had failed to do it, and now everybody was going to suffer. Motomaniax were billed as a major attraction on the programmes, which were being printed, and on the posters, which were already printed, some already on display.

'I'm sorry.'

'You can say sorry till you're blue in the face,' Dad said, 'it's not going to make any difference, is it? Now clear out before I do something I may really regret.'

Grace cleared out and went upstairs. Her happy network of coincidences had collapsed. After Dizzy mentioned Fate she had begun to make a list: If I hadn't been home last Friday night Steffi wouldn't have asked for the telescope. If I hadn't gone up in the loft with it I wouldn't have seen the knight. If I hadn't been searching for the knight I wouldn't have met Dizzy and Salvo wouldn't be using the wheeling machine. There was one more now, that wrecked everything: If I hadn't borrowed the map I'd have left that letter on the table where Dad would have found it at once.

She hadn't caused the disaster; that had happened in Sunderland, but she had made it much worse. Would she be grounded again, just when everything was starting to happen? Would she have to stay at home and watch Frank and Salvo rushing off to make armour and mudguards, taking over *her* friends? She had been sure that Mum was coming round to the idea of letting her go where she liked. How could she explain to Dizzy?

The Lincoln began hooting in the hall. It couldn't be Dizzy yet. She leaned over the banisters just in case and watched Dad's bald spot as he went to answer it.

'Hullo? Oh, hullo. No, haven't seen him . . . haven't a clue . . . no, sorry. Goodbye. Yes, I'll tell him. Yes, goodbye. No, I haven't. No. Goodbye.'

He went back to the office. That must have been Venetia. She had had so many similar conversations with Venetia over the phone, as Venetia pursued Salvo around town from the comfort of her own living room. If Venetia wasn't careful she was going to lose Salvo. Grace thought of him last night, talking peacefully with Birgitta in the Morleys' kitchen.

She crept downstairs again and went out to the garage, where Frank was measuring up the remains of the rear mudguards.

'We're going to work some more on the first one tonight,' he said. 'You did us a good turn there, Auntie. Let's be frank,' he said, 'we do have a talent for knowing the right people.'

We? Grace thought. 'Will it be ready in time for the rally?'

'Dunno. Hope so. If we work flat out . . .' He looked up. 'What's the matter with you?'

'I've done something awful,' Grace said, 'when I was sorting out the letters last week. I left an important one on top of the bookcase and Dad's only just found it. It was from Motomaniax. They've cancelled. Some of them have had an accident and they can't do it.'

'Can't do what?'

'The rally. They were the special event.'

'You mean you've wrecked the rally single-handed? Congratulations.'

'I haven't wrecked it.'

'No, there's just going to be a stonking great hole in the middle. I suppose the posters have gone out. And the programmes are at the printers.'

'I've never done anything like that before.'

'Well, you only have to do it once,' said Frank. Grace turned away. It was no good. He wasn't going to say anything to make her feel better.

The Lincoln was hooting again. It stopped and then she heard Dad shouting, 'Auntie! For you!' She ran indoors. The top of the Lincoln was lying on its back beside the chassis, like a stranded beetle. Grace picked it up.

'Dizzy?'

'No, it's me, man. You going to see Dizzy this afternoon?'

'I don't know,' Grace said, dolefully. 'I might not be let.'

'Oh, man, what you done now?'

She knew Dad could overhear her. 'I'll tell you later. Why d'you want to know about Dizzy?'

'I got to take the van back to the yard when I get home from Gareth's place. Then I'm seeing Venetia. If you go up to St Dunstan's, can you take the mudguard sections with you? Save me coming back for them. The ones I cut to size – Frank knows where they are.'

'I'll try,' Grace said. 'Venetia rang just now. If she calls again, shall I tell her where you are?'

'No thank you – and stay out of trouble, hey, Auntie?' Salvo pleaded. 'You too valuable to lose.'

It had to be Salvo, of course, who was the one to say something kind. Now she felt she could face Dad again. She went into the office.

'Dad? I'm really sorry.'

'What are you after?' Dad said.

'Are you going to ground me again?'

'No,' Dad said, 'If I ground you you'll be under my feet all day, reminding me.'

'If I get asked out, can I go?'

'I'd advise you to go,' Dad said. He still hadn't looked up. 'The more distance you put between us right now, the better I shall like it.'

When the Lincoln hooted again Grace was still in the hall, and pounced on it.

'Dizzy?'

It was Mum. 'Expect me when you see me. Rachel may have started.'

'Started what?'

'The baby. It's two weeks early but you never know. She's got a pain, anyway, tell Dad. And tell Helen when she gets in; she might want to come over.'

Grace hung up again. Already Mum would be dialling Lynette's number, and they would all make a beeline for Gavin and Rachel's, ready for the baby: Helen, Lynette, Rachel's mum, Rachel's sister Kate. The house would fill up with the sisters and the grannies, all except for her. She would be left hanging around on the edge with the brothers and the grandpas. By the time she got round to having a baby everyone else would be too old to care.

Expect me when you see me. When would it be her turn to make airy farewells like that and head for the horizon?

The Lincoln went off under her elbow, *kadookah!* This time she just gave the number and waited.

'Grace?'

'Dizzy?'

'That was quick. Were you waiting?'

'Of course I was.'

'Can you come over this afternoon?'

'Yes.' Well, she had been more or less ordered out of the house.

'Daddy'll come and collect you. Two o'clock? Don't eat much lunch; Birgitta's making us a picnic.'

Grace went into the office.

'Now what?' Dad was hammering envelopes shut with the side of his hand.

'Mum says Rachel's started so she won't be back yet. And my friend's coming to pick me up at two. Is that all right?'

'Are they bringing you home again?'

'Yes.'

'And when can we expect you?'

Grace longed to say, When you see me. 'I don't know. Can I ring?'

'Tell me a time and stick to it,' Dad said. 'There might not be anyone home when you ring.'

'Nine-thirty?' Grace said daringly.

'Are you winding me up?'

'I mean nine-thirty at the very latest. I might be much earlier.'

'Seven-thirty,' Dad said. 'That's quite late enough.'

'I won't be on my own –'

'Quite late enough for a girl in my bad books. Do you want to argue or do you want to go out?' Dad laid into another envelope.

'Dad, I'm really sorry about the letter. I'm really really sorry . . .'

He looked up at last. 'I know you are,' he said. 'But being sorry doesn't help, does it?'

At five to two Grace collected the cut-outs from Frank and went to stand by the gate. Salvo knew what he was doing, but if she had not seen for herself what the wheeling machine could perform it would have been hard to believe that these flat shapes could ever become a mudguard. They looked and handled like frozen fish fillets.

Steffi and Sarah were coming round the side of the Milners' house. Steffi called across the road.

'We're going up the hill. D'you want to come?'

Grace was under no illusions about Steffi's budding friendliness. Suddenly Grace had something that Steffi wanted; not something like the telescope that could be demanded, but something that had to be got at by subtle means. Like Gareth, for instance. Poor old Steffi, Grace thought, with a superior smile that she did not allow to show. She had already worked out that Gareth must be a lot older than he looked; in any case, he was more or less married.

'No thank you,' Grace said, 'I'm getting a lift.' As she said it she saw, and Steffi saw, a BMW turning up the Close. Frank heard it, and came bounding out of the garage to look. He could recognize cars by their engine note and he was not going to miss this one. Sarah, Grace noticed, gave him a quick glance which did not linger. Evidently Frank had fallen from favour.

Dizzy was out of the car almost before it had parked, already talking.

'. . . you get those metal things, Daddy. Hullo, Frank, are you coming with us? Is that your friend with the loft?'

Mr Morley got out of the car obediently. Grace caught hold of Dizzy before she could rush across the road and start talking to Steffi. Dizzy might well ask Steffi and Sarah to come with them, she was so desperate to meet people. She might ask to go and see the loft, suggest they fetched the telescope. Mr Morley would not intervene, Grace was sure. It was Mummy who gave orders; Daddy seemed happy to fall in with what anyone else wanted.

'Where's Salvo?' he said.

'Over at Gareth's,' Frank said. 'He'll be up later, about four. I'll get along when I can.'

'Is he working this afternoon?'

'Nah, he's putting in a couple of hours with his girl,' Frank said. 'He's only got the van when he's working. He sold his bike to buy the Fordson. Now she wants him to sell the Fordson and buy a car.'

'Is that it? Can I have a look?' Mr Morley laid

the fish fillets on the gatepost and followed Frank into the garage.

Grace turned to Dizzy. 'Does your mum know I'm coming up?'

Dizzy shook her head. 'I don't know. She's away today.' She lowered her voice. 'She and Daddy had a humungous row last night, after you'd gone.'

'About us?' The Charters next door had terrible rows. You could hear them through the party wall along with the occasional crash if Mrs Charter threw something. Grace could not quite imagine Mummy throwing things.

'Not just you; the wheeling machine, and Salvo, and Gareth. She doesn't like Gareth. She thinks he's useless. That's what he says, too. He doesn't mind. "I'm the no-good younger brother," he says.'   ·

'Sounds like Frank,' said Grace.

Mr Morley came out of the garage. 'Ready?' he said, seeing them hovering. He picked up the fillets and Grace and Dizzy followed him to the car, Grace wondering if he had overheard what Dizzy was saying. She did not like to think that she had been partly the cause of a row between Dizzy's parents; on the other hand, if Mummy didn't like Salvo and Gareth, she would rather not be the kind of person that Mummy did like. She didn't even seem to like Dizzy very much.

Chapter Ten

*T*hey sat in the sun at the feet of Georgiana Ledbetter and ate Birgitta's picnic. Picnics at home involved hardboiled eggs, packets of crisps, and bread rolls crammed into ice-cream cartons so that they came out square. Birgitta had packed a real wicker basket with salads and fresh fruit, smoked fish and little crumbly pastries. Everything was wrapped in cloth napkins. Each time Dizzy dived into the basket Grace thought they must have reached the last napkin, but there was always something more until they had worked their way down to the wicker and found a sheet of paper with THE END printed on it.

'Birgitta's nice, isn't she?' Grace said, thinking of the time she must have spent preparing the basket and knowing who was going to have to iron the napkins.

'Yes. I hope she stays,' Dizzy said, as though she thought that unlikely.

'Where's your mum?'

'She's gone to a wedding in Cheltenham,' Dizzy said. 'She won't be back till tomorrow night. I think the Blessed Damozel must have sent her there. I asked her to make something good happen, at the end of term, and she's working overtime. Daddy's home for a whole month, that's why Gareth's here such a lot. He hardly ever comes when Daddy's away. Trouble is, there's so many things I want, I don't like to ask for too much in case she goes on strike.'

'Things?' What could Dizzy want that she didn't already have?

'Oh, *firstly*,' Dizzy began ticking off items on her fingers, 'firstly, I wish Daddy would work in England, secondly, I wish I didn't have to go to Silsbury Hall House, thirdly, I wish Birgitta would stay with us, fourthly, I wish I could see Gareth and Marian whenever I like, and nextly I wish I could see *you* whenever I like —'

Grace was touched, but she could see why Dizzy was afraid that the Blessed Damozel might throw in the towel.

'What's Silsbury Hall House?'

'My school,' Dizzy said.

'I've never heard of it.'

'It's near Rye.'

'*Rye?*' Rye was not even in Kent. 'You go there every day?'

'Every week,' Dizzy said. 'I come home at weekends. I hate it. Some people just hate it on the first day, the ones who board all term, and then they cry when they have to go home. I hate it all the time. I want to come home every night.'

'Why do you go there, then?'

'Mummy says there aren't any good schools round here, but I bet there's a good school nearer than Rye.'

'What does Daddy say?' Grace asked sharply.

'He wouldn't mind where I went, but he's away so much. I wish I could go to Wing Farm with you. I bet that's a good school. We'd see each other all the time.'

'Well, we can in the holidays,' Grace said. 'Like now.'

'Only because the Blessed Damozel sent Mummy to Cheltenham,' Dizzy said.

It occurred to Grace that Dizzy did not seem to like Mummy much, either. It must be a strange way to live. Did she herself like Mum and Dad, or Frank and Helen, come to that? They were hers, she was theirs. Even if they quarrelled and complained, if she got into trouble, was punished, forgiven, liking didn't come into it. Lynette and Gavin and Alison might be adults that she scarcely knew, but they were still her brothers and sisters. She never thought about *liking* them. Perhaps Dizzy did not think about it either, simply took it for granted that she and her mother had nothing in common and that it was just bad luck that one of them sort of owned the other.

'Have you tried praying?'

'What, instead of wishing?' Dizzy reached out for the left foot of the Blessed Damozel and gave it a reassuring pat. 'Do you believe in God, then?'

'Not really,' Grace said. 'Just thought it might work better than wishing.'

'Neither do I,' Dizzy said, adding shrewdly, 'but you can't say so, can you?'

Through the gap in the garden wall they saw Birgitta coming along the grass path between the flowerbeds.

'Someone's going out,' Grace said.

'Who?' Dizzy stared. 'Birgitta's got Monday off, not today.'

'Why's she all done up, then?' Birgitta was wearing a floaty white cotton shirt over a long velvet skirt, and her hair was combed out like a veil over her shoulders. Even from a distance they could see that she was very carefully made up.

'You look nice,' Dizzy said.

'The mouse is playing,' Birgitta said obscurely. 'Are you enjoying my picnic?' She saw the empty basket. 'You are enjoyed?'

'Cosmic,' Grace said, which was Salvo's favourite compliment. 'What mouse?'

'While the cat is awaying . . .' Birgitta explained. 'Now, Salvo is coming at four o'clock and also Frank is, while he can, and so we are wheeling in the shed and Mr Morley is saying when is Grace going home?'

Grace suddenly appreciated what Salvo had

144

meant when he said that Birgitta lived in the present.

'I've got to be back by half-past seven. I'll go with Frank and Salvo.'

'I think Salvo and Frank is staying more than that,' Birgitta said, as if she were sure of it. 'Mr Morley is taking you home, don't worry. I am making tea while Salvo is coming.'

She tripped away again. Birgitta seemed to know a lot about Salvo's movements, Grace thought.

Everyone who was tall enough took a turn at assisting Salvo with the mudguard. Dizzy and Grace went outside and watched through the window to leave more room in the workshop. One after the other Mr Morley, Gareth and Frank joined in the rock and roll of the wheeling machine. Then Salvo turned to Birgitta, who was looking on from the doorway. They could not hear what he said but they saw Birgitta nod, start forward and then pause, looking down at her white shirt.

'Doesn't want to get dirt on her clothes,' Dizzy said. 'How *girlie.*'

Apparently Salvo persuaded her that there was no dirt involved, for she took Frank's place opposite Salvo, and then it turned into a dance indeed, although the steel was becoming an odd shape.

Afterwards they went into the house. Dizzy's father opened big floor-length windows in the living room and they all sat round on a paved terrace outside. There was a striking clock somewhere in the house. Grace listened to it carving away the hour by quarters, aware that someone soon would say, 'Time you were getting home, Auntie'; aware that if they did not she would have to say something herself. She would not risk Dad's wrath by being late, but it would be so hard to leave, knowing that the others would go on sitting there talking, drinking, laughing, while the sun went down and warm darkness fell about them. It was like being in a picture. When she left there would be a white space where she had been sitting.

'We been talking,' Salvo announced, from where he was sitting with Birgitta. It was Birgitta he had been talking to. 'We'll walk home with Auntie and then come back here. If we start now we'll be back at the Close by half-past. You ready, Auntie?'

'I'll come with you!' Dizzy said, starting to scramble to her feet, but her father put his hand on her shoulder and said something very quietly. 'Oh!' Dizzy said. 'All right. I'll see you off. I'll race you down to the fence.'

Grace followed her but they stopped running as soon as they were out of earshot.

'What's going on?' Grace said. 'I thought your dad —'

'Ssssh!' Dizzy was having one of her giggling fits. 'It's a plot, Salvo and Birgitta. They want to see you home so they can walk back together.'

After that Grace was afraid that they would be holding hands and swoon-swooning over each other while she was left to tag along behind, but

Birgitta and Salvo walked on either side of her, in single file along the narrow path. When they reached the road they all linked hands and swung down the hill in step, one-two-three-*kick*.

'Oh, man, that Gareth, that septic tank,' Salvo sang. 'Auntie, you'll love it. We all going out there on Wednesday, see the Company practise.'

'What is septic tank?' Birgitta said.

'You don't want to know,' Salvo assured her. 'It is a strange and secret subterranean thing understood only by plumbers.' Grace suspected that Birgitta understood about one-tenth of what Salvo said, not that it seemed to matter. 'And Gareth's lady. She's a witch for sure.'

'A real witch?'

'She got a real witch's kitchen. Bunches of herbs and crystals hanging in the window, and scented candles all around. And she dress in string.'

'String?'

'You'll see.'

'What about Hendrickje?'

'Hendrickje's a fine figure of a mare. And they got a little donkey. And goats – you ever tasted curried goat? It's heaven, man.'

'I thought it was a farm,' Grace said.

'It's a cattery. A holiday home for pussy cats,' Salvo said. 'It used to be a farm, but it look like shanty town now. Wait till you see it. Wait till your dad see it. Sir Gareth of shanty town. No wonder the ugly sister can't stand him.'

'Who is the ugly sister?' Birgitta said.

'Hmmm,' said Salvo.

As they turned the corner at the foot of the hill

147

a car drew in to the kerb. It looked only vaguely familiar until Grace saw Mum leaning out of the window on the passenger side. The driver was her brother Gavin. She broke free of Birgitta and Salvo and ran to the car.

'Niece or nephew?'

'False alarm,' Mum said. 'Panic over. What on earth are you doing?'

'Just coming home.'

'And who's that with Salvo?'

'Birgitta. We told you about Birgitta. They're seeing me home.'

'You'd better get in the back,' Mum said. 'They look like they've got something better to do.'

On Wednesday evening Salvo borrowed the Thompson Vauxhall and they drove out to the farm. Grace sat in the back with Frank and Dizzy. Birgitta sat up front beside Salvo. Salvo was explaining how a septic tank worked and Birgitta was staring at him as though he were describing sunrise over the Himalayas.

In a lane on the outskirts of a scattered village they turned on to a drive beside a paddock where a tall, solid black horse was grazing peaceably beside a woolly donkey, and three goats stared over the fence with yellow eyes. Beyond the paddock stood a brick barn and at an angle to the barn was a low, lumpy-looking house with a hunched roof.

'That's where the cats live, in the barn,' Dizzy was saying. 'It's lovely in there, they've got central heating and all the pens have little gardens at the back and Marian goes and talks to them so that they don't think nobody loves them any more. I wish Silsbury Hall House was a cattery,' she said, and trailed off into silence as the car stopped.

That must be Marian coming out to meet them. Salvo had been right when he said that she dressed in string. Everything that she was wearing was loosely knitted out of undyed yarn. Perhaps she had spun it herself. It was sheep-coloured, except for a long orange scarf draped round her shoulders. Dizzy clambered over Grace to be out of the car first, and hurled herself at Marian yammering, 'This is my friend Grace and this is her brother and that's Salvo —'

'I've met Salvo,' Marian said. She and Birgitta seemed to know each other already; they were hugging and laughing. In their long hair and long dresses – or whatever the garment was that Marian was wearing – they looked, Grace thought, like ladies from some distant time, waiting at a castle gate for their knight.

'Where's Gareth?' she said.

'Hullo, Grace,' Marian said. 'Hullo, Frank. Gareth's out with the others, they've already started. Go round to the back. Dizzy knows the way.'

Salvo had gone back to chat to the goats. Grace followed Dizzy across a little patch of garden in the angle of the barn and the house. Herbs and lavender grew in the beds between gravel paths and from an apple tree a wind chime hung. Vines grew against the wall. It was nothing like any shanty town that Grace had ever seen on the news. What had Salvo been talking about? Then they went through a gate in the wall, and she found out.

Behind the wall was a muddy enclosure that had once been a farmyard. It was bordered on both sides by wooden pens and cinder-block sheds whose sheet-iron roofs had collapsed and slid to the ground as though a hurricane had recently passed over. A very primitive tractor stood in one corner, behind a rampart of blackened straw bales with a squat tower of motor tyres at one end.

'Come on.' Dizzy, skittering across the mud on a causeway of ashes, turned to beckon, but Grace slowed down for a closer look. Among all the rust and rot she saw familiar outlines: a cake mill, a potato riddler, a cylinder that might be the boiler of a stationary engine. Did Gareth know what he had here? No wonder Salvo thought Dad would love it.

She could hear a regular clanging sound and wondered if one of the machines might be working; then Dizzy steered her round a horsebox, collapsed on perished tyres, and they came out of shanty town into a meadow. It sloped gently downhill between hawthorn hedges, and on the sunlit grass ten or a dozen men were hacking at each other with swords.

'The Company of the White Horse,' Dizzy said proudly.

Grace, still haunted by her first sight of Gareth through the telescope, had expected to see men in armour, but most of them were wearing padded tunics with steel plates on the chest and chainmail on their legs. Their heads were all enclosed by what Grace had learned to identify as bascinets. It was their facelessness that was frightening, not their weapons.

'Which one's Gareth?' Grace said.

'The one in the helm,' Dizzy said. 'Nobody else has got one.'

'I thought he'd be on his horse.'

'I told you, he doesn't fight on Hendrickje,' Dizzy said. 'That was Hendrickje out at the front with Jenny – she's the donkey.'

'That big horse with hairy legs, that's Hendrickje?' Grace had imagined that a knight's horse would be a graceful, prancing creature. 'But that's a carthorse!'

'A heavy horse,' Dizzy corrected her. 'She's a Friesian; she's Dutch, that's why she's called Hendrickje. Destriers had to be heavy horses – think of the weight they had to carry. Think of the great helm. I can't even lift it.'

Grace also remembered Dad describing a knight as a one-man tank. Of course he would need something the size of Hendrickje.

'He just rides ahead of the Company on her; she's too old to train, and he'd never risk her getting hurt,' Dizzy said.

'They don't hurt each other, do they? Aren't they just pretending?'

'Oh, no,' Dizzy said. 'They're really fighting.'

'Those are real swords?' It looked real enough. Gareth and his opponent seemed to be trying to saw each other's heads off. Helm and bascinet met with a jarring clang.

'They're real but they aren't sharp. They're not actually trying to kill each other,' Dizzy explained, redundantly. 'When there's a proper battle there's sometimes forty of them crashing about, they couldn't use edged weapons. People do get hurt though. Didn't you see that scar on Gareth's neck?'

The warriors were gradually grinding to a halt, standing at ease or lolling on the grass. One lifted the visor of his bascinet and lit a pipe. No one seemed to have been injured or even slightly dented.

Gareth eased off his helm and came over to them. 'Want to try it?' he said, handing Grace his sword. She had expected it to be heavy but she was pulled off-balance by the weight.

'Doesn't it hurt?'

'It would if I really laid on with it,' Gareth said, 'but we pull the blows.' He took the sword back. 'Look, I hold it quite loosely –' he brought the blade down in a swishing arc against his own leg '– and then just before it makes contact I tighten my grip and that softens the impact. And it isn't edged – it's not sharpened. Some of us have little private combats with edged weapons, but never when we're staging a battle. And we're all in armour. It really does work; it's not just for show.'

Gareth was clad from head to foot in chainmail, made up of thousands of little metal rings, like iron knitting, with a tunic over the top. Great chainmail gauntlets covered his hands, turning them into bear's paws, and on his legs and arms, over the mail, were plates of steel armour.

'You could make those on the wheeling machine,' Grace said.

'That's what we thought, though since we learned how to use it we're not so sure.' He put his gauntlets into the great helm and stood it upside down on the grass. Grace surreptitiously nudged it with her foot, but it did not even rock. It was lined with some kind of fur, but she blenched to think of him carrying that weight on his *head*.

'Don't stub your toe,' Gareth said.

'Did you make the chainmail?'

'No, I bought that from John St Leger,' Gareth began, but Dizzy broke in.

'Oh no, don't say that. Tell her the *story*.'

'OK. I stripped it from the corpse I slew myself at the Battle of Poitiers; that would have been in 1356, when the Black Prince led us against the French. The helm I nicked from a new-slain knight, foully murdered by renegades and lying in a ditch. The greaves —' he tapped his shin with the sword, '— I bought from a bowman who'd looted more than he could wear.'

'He's going into business,' said a voice behind them. Marian had come out with Frank and Salvo and Birgitta. 'He's got the horse, he's got the helm, he's got the armour and the sword. Now he's going to gather a mob of mindless thugs around him and go maurauding through France.'

'What so historical about that, man?' Salvo said. ''Ere we go, 'ere we go, 'ere we go . . .'

'Yes, but this is the Hundred Years War,' Gareth said. 'Philip of Burgundy has signed the Treaty of Bretigny with Edward III of England.

Edward has ordered his knights to come home, but that leaves thousands of armed men milling around Europe with nothing to do and no way of earning a living. So what do we do? We call ourselves Free Companies and we fight for anyone who will hire us. If nobody hires us we fight anyway. A man's got to eat.'

'We?' Frank said.

'The Company of the White Horse; soldiers of fortune. Motto: We Loot and Pillage.'

'It keeps them off the streets,' Marian murmured.

'Not one member of this company has a criminal record,' Gareth said loftily. 'Well, not for anything physical; no assault and battery or aggravated wounding, nothing like that. Tom Sellars got done for speeding, but that's about the worst. All the aggro takes place on the field of battle and anyway, remember the watchword: Never in Anger. Got to get back now. Carl wants to go night-clubbing.'

'He's going to a night club?' Salvo said. 'Dressed like that? Tell me which one, I feel I belong there.'

'*K*night-clubbing,' Marian said. 'Clubbing knights. It's a very effective technique. You get your club – it's a sledgehammer handle studded with iron bolts – and bash your knight on his plate armour, just above the knee. That dents the armour and makes the joint seize up; result, one knight out of commission. It's the medieval equivalent of putting sugar in the petrol tank. Look, I don't find this terribly exciting, to tell you the truth. Does anyone want to come and have a drink? No, I can see nobody does. You'd rather slake your bloodlust.'

Marian turned away and began to walk back alone across the muddy yard.

'I'd like a drink, please,' Grace said, running after her. Everyone else was watching the warriors join battle again, but she was afraid that Marian might feel hurt; and she was beginning to get the first faint tickling of a good idea. She had a few questions to ask Marian before she could be sure that it *was* a good idea.

Chapter Eleven

Marian's kitchen smelled of smoke and warm wax and lavender. Although it was summer a wood fire burned in a hearth that was big enough to stand up in, and the ceiling was so low that the bunches of herbs that hung from a drying rack were at head height. Grace felt them scrape her hair as she walked underneath. There were little cramped windows in unexpected places, and crystals hung on threads against the glass, turning slowly, making rainbows on the white walls and stone floor. Candles stood everywhere.

'She's a witch for sure,' Salvo had said. What

was she going to offer by way of a drink?

Marian switched on a corner light by pulling a length of string that hung by the fireplace. There was a fridge at the back of the kitchen, under a tiled worktop, and on the worktop was an electric kettle and a jar of instant coffee.

'I'm having de-caff,' Marian said. 'Same for you?'

'Please.' Grace sat down at the table, which was almost as big as the one in the Morleys' kitchen and covered with a green blanket. Marian brought the coffee and before she sat down lit a fat wax candle that stood in a dish of sand in the middle of the table.

'Companionable,' Marian said. Grace nodded. 'You must be the girl who saw Gareth through the telescope.'

'That's right,' Grace said.

'Pure chance,' Marian said. 'He very rarely goes down there, but with Bill being home – Dizzy's father – he's making up for lost time.'

'Dizzy said.'

'Dizzy doesn't miss much. They were taking photographs that evening. That's why he had the armour on. He doesn't usually run around with it in public, except when they're staging a battle.'

'Yes, battles,' Grace said. 'Do they really do them in public?'

'Oh, sure,' Marian said. 'People part with hard cash to watch.'

'Don't you like the Company?' Grace said, detecting a lack of enthusiasm.

'I don't really see the point,' Marian said. 'If

157

they want to charge around in the mud and hack each other about and then go off to the pub, why don't they join a Rugby club?'

'Being soldiers of fortune is more fun, I expect,' Grace suggested.

'Marginally less chance of losing your front teeth, anyway. And now Gareth wants to make armour for Hendrickje. At the moment he's a poor knight –'

'I've heard about them.'

'Apparently poor knights didn't bother with horse armour, but now he plans to be a real knight, one of the goodies. He'll still charge about hacking people to death, of course, but in a good cause,' Marian said.

Grace hoped that she was not going to say anything unkind about Gareth. She did not want to hear. She was beginning to like Marian and did not want to find herself having to take sides. 'But they're not like that really, are they?' she said.

'No. That's what I can't understand. You couldn't find a nicer bunch of guys, and yet they're pretending to be some of the most horrible people in the history of Europe. Still,' Marian said thoughtfully, 'anyone who has anything to do with re-enactment tends to be slightly eccentric.'

'Re-enactment?'

'That's what it's called: re-enactment of battles. Sometimes it's real battles like, well, Tewkesbury, during the Wars of the Roses. Do you know about that? Battle of Bosworth, Stamford Bridge, Edge-hill, Battle of Hastings . . .'

'How do they get enough people?'

'Different companies get together,' Marian said. 'It's not just our mob. There's hundreds of these groups – companies, though companies are usually medieval – all over the country; all over the world, believe it or not: Romans, Vikings, Dark Ages, Cavaliers, Roundheads; some of those Vikings are really wild. They call each other up: Let's have a battle, the way you or I might ask friends round for lunch, and off they go. They invent some excuse, you know, tax-gathering or horse stealing. I go along sometimes to swell the numbers,' Marian sighed. 'Dame Marian and Sir Gareth.'

'But where do they fight?' Grace said, sure now that her idea was not just good but brilliant, a face-saver if not a life-saver.

'Anywhere. Out in the meadow, most of the time. Tewkesbury, if it's the Battle of Tewkesbury. At fêtes –'

'That's it,' Grace broke in. 'They go to fêtes. Can you book them?'

'Well, people do,' Marian said. 'You don't want to book them, do you?'

'Do you think they'd do a steam rally?'

'You're serious,' Marian said, wonderingly. 'Have some more coffee. Tell me what's going on. But don't tell me you're running a steam rally.'

'Not me,' Grace said, 'my dad. He's running it, the Arling Valley Steam and Transport Bonanza, at Arling airfield. And Frank and Salvo are entering this old lorry –'

'A *steam* lorry?'

'No, petrol. You don't have to run off steam to

159

be in the rally. That's why they needed the wheeling machine, to make the mudguards on. And after I saw Gareth through the telescope I went to look for him, only I needed a map to find out where he would be and I had this letter for Dad that said that the stunt team who were going to come to the rally *couldn't* come, only I left it on a shelf and Dad didn't find it for ages.'

'Slow down, slow down,' Marian said. 'What stunt team?'

'There's always something special at the rally. This team ride motorbikes and jump through hoops and that – fiery hoops, you know – and form pyramids, and ride blindfold.'

'My god,' Marian said, 'and I thought our lot were doolally.'

'But they can't come and now it's too late to find anyone else. And it's my fault.'

'And you think Gareth and the Company might like to lay on something?'

Grace felt discouraged. 'Do you think they would? Would they like to?'

'Would they *like* to?'

'We pay,' Grace said.

'If I know Gareth, he'd probably pay *you*,' Marian said. She went over to a calendar hanging above the sink. 'They don't seem to be booked to slaughter anyone for a week or two. Tewkesbury's the 27th. When's your rally?'

'Weekend after next, 13th and 14th August.'

'And does your father know about this?'

'I only thought of it just now,' Grace admitted. 'What should we do, ask Gareth first, or tell Dad?'

'Let's think this out.' Marian sat down again. 'Personally I should think they'd be delighted, but do we ask them first and risk your father saying no, or do we tell your father and risk Gareth saying no? A very *slight* risk.'

'Do you think he will?'

'Not a chance,' Marian said. 'Not a chance he'll say no. But your father might, yes?'

'Well, he doesn't know anything about the Company. I never told him. Frank might have.'

'Don't you tell them where you're going?'

'Frank doesn't have to. They know where I am, but nobody really cares what I do,' Grace said. 'I mean, they don't mind what I do so long as they know where I am and I'm not home late.'

'So you could be out joy-riding or worrying sheep?'

Grace felt ashamed. 'It's not like that,' she said, 'but everybody else is grown up. Helen's the next to me and she's seventeen. It's not they don't care, it's just –'

'Just that they've all forgotten what it's like?' Marian smiled, unexpectedly. 'Well, Grace, I'm twice as old as your Helen, but I must say I find you very good company. Now, is your father home at the moment?'

'He will be by the time I get back.'

'Hasn't it gone quiet?' Marian said. Grace realized that while they were talking peacefully in the peaceful kitchen the distant sounds of battle had died away. 'They'll be in here to change, in a minute. Look, ask your father what he thinks when you get home, and I'll ask Gareth what *he* thinks, when you've gone, and then I'll ring you and we can take it from there. All right?'

'Cosmic,' Grace said.

Salvo ran her home.

'I suppose you're going back again,' Grace said, knowing that he was. Dizzy and Frank and Birgitta were still at the farm. She had thought that Dizzy might show solidarity by going home too, but forgave her, seeing how happy she was with Gareth and Marian.

'Auntie, don't rush things,' Salvo said. 'Your horizons widening daily, man. Haven't you noticed? Two weeks ago you didn't know any of these crazy people. No one in the family got friends like you got, Auntie.'

'Yes, but you can see them whenever you like,' Grace said. 'I can't. I only get to see them because they're your friends too.'

'If we can get Ron and Jacquie up to see that yard, man, you won't be able to keep them away either,' Salvo said. 'Then all your problems be over. Meantime, my wheels is your command, while I got wheels, that is. I take you anywhere you want to go, any time. I'm in your debt, Auntie. You found me the wheeling machine, you found Birgitta —'

'What about Venetia?' Grace said, crushingly.

'Venetia let me know one time too many that I'm not good enough for her,' Salvo said. 'This time, I agreed.'

No more phonecalls, Grace thought. 'Are you going to join the Company?'

'Sure thing, baby.'

'Just making armour?'

'No, man, I'm going to *fight*. Anyway, we have to rethink the whole armour scene. Turns out armour is all different thicknesses; like that helm; almost twice as thick on top. Well, the helm's OK, it's all made of separate pieces, but a breast-plate – we couldn't wheel that.'

'But I thought you *were* going to be armourers.'

'We are,' Salvo said. 'But we're going to learn to do it properly; we assume the mantle of John James St Leger. Maybe we'll run up a small coat of plates for Gareth on the wheeling machine.'

Dad was already home when Salvo dropped her at the gate. He was looking at his watch.

'But I'm *early*,' Grace protested, as Salvo drove away.

'I know, I know. Can't a man look at his watch now and again? Want anything to eat?'

'I've had something,' Grace said, waiting for him to ask where she had been, but he didn't. She was home on time, that was all that mattered.

She followed him into the house. 'Dad?'

'What are you after?'

'I'm not after anything. I want to help.'

'I think I've had enough of your help, Auntie.'

'That's what I meant. Have you found anyone for the steam rally?'

'Instead of Motomaniax? No, I haven't. Not likely to either.'

'I think I have,' Grace said.

He didn't believe her, she could tell. 'Like who?'

'You know my friends, the ones I go to see up at St Dunstan's?'

'I thought you were out at Sternham.'

'That was just tonight.' She knew how difficult it would be to explain everything that had happened during the last fortnight and decided not to try. She might let slip something about the telescope. 'My friends do re-enactment.'

'How much?'

'Re-enactment. They dress up as knights and soldiers, in armour, and fight battles, like in the Middle Ages. It's real weapons and armour, and they really fight. It's not like on telly, with actors.'

'Kill each other as well, do they?' He still wasn't taking her seriously.

'No, they don't. It's very skilled.' She tried to recall what Gareth had told her. 'They pull their blows.'

'Sounds painful.'

'*Dad*. They do it at fêtes and rallies and –'

'Hang about. Are you suggesting we have this mob up at Arling?'

'You could ask them,' Grace said. 'They'd put on a real battle and they aren't doing anything that weekend. Someone's phoning me in a minute to say if they will.'

'Do you mean to say you've already fixed this up? Without asking me?' Now he was getting cross again, possibly about to be furious. 'Have you gone and invited them –?'

'No, no I haven't. But I didn't know who to ask first, you or them.'

'Me,' Dad said firmly. 'You ask me first.'

'I didn't want to tell you until I knew if they could, and I didn't want to ask them in case you said they couldn't. It's not fair,' Grace shouted. 'I can't do anything right.'

'Calm down. Calm down.' Dad pulled her on to his knee. It was a long time since she had sat on his lap. She leaned against his shoulder. 'Now listen, Auntie. You know how big this rally is; there will be thousands of people there. They're expecting real entertainment, something worth paying for, not a bunch of idiots, amateurs, banging each other over the head with rubber battle-axes.'

'They don't,' Grace said. 'It *is* real, the weapons are real, the armour's real, they really fight. I saw them this evening. They're not idiots.'

Dad thought about it for a bit. 'They could put on a big show, could they?'

'Yes. A real combat.'

'And it looks as if they're really killing each other? People might like that . . .'

The Lincoln honked, *kadookah! kadookah!*

'That's for me,' Grace said, running for the hall.

'Grace?' It was Marian. 'I thought I'd better warn you. Gareth's on his way. I just happened to suggest that there might be a chance that the Company could fight at your steam rally and I'm afraid there was no holding him after that. Have you managed to have a word with your father yet?'

'He's just starting to say yes.' Grace went shivery at the thought of how nearly he had said no. If she hadn't kept on at him he might have refused even to think about it. What would have happened then when Gareth turned up? She ought to have confided in Salvo. Salvo could talk anybody into anything. 'Is it just Gareth coming?'

'Dizzy and Frank are with him. Salvo's gone off to the Green Man with Birgitta and I can't leave the cats. I'll see you soon. If not before, we'll meet at Arling.'

It sounded like a battle cry: *We'll meet at Arling*!

Gareth arrived about ten minutes later, which suggested that the Big Healey had not been hanging about. Frank went straight to the garage but Dizzy rapped on the back door and bounced in without waiting for anybody to answer. Gareth followed, carrying a box file. He and Dad stood raising their eyebrows at each other until Grace, remembering that they had not met before, introduced them.

'Dad, this is my friend Dizzy and this is her Uncle Gareth and this is my dad. Gareth's in the Company of the White Horse.'

'Good evening,' Dad said. 'In what?'

'It's our re-enactment society,' Gareth said. 'Our period's the mid-fourteenth century. We rampage through Europe.'

'Pleased to meet you. I'm Ron Thompson and I'm retired from the Post Office,' Dad said. 'Have a seat. Coffee, Auntie. Or would you rather have tea? Auntie tells me that you wouldn't mind staging a full-scale battle at our steam rally. I have to admit,' Dad said heavily, 'I'm not at all sure I like the sound of it.'

'You've never seen re-enactment?' Gareth said. 'I've brought some visuals —'

'They're brilliant!' Dizzy burst out. 'It's just like real. You'd think they'd had a camera in 1360, you know, like taking pictures for the papers.'

'All right,' Dad said. 'Auntie, why don't you and your friend go upstairs or out in the garden while we sort this out?'

'Dizzy, shut up!' Grace hissed. She was not going to stand by and let Dad turn the Company into an exclusive, grown-up affair, shutting her out. 'I want to see the pictures.'

Dad had his I'm-not-arguing look. Grace thought of the conversation in the car with Salvo.

'They're *my* friends,' she said.

'So they are,' Dad said unexpectedly. 'OK, you stay. But keep the noise level down.'

Gareth was spreading the table with photographs. Some were snapshots, others blown up almost to poster size. Even after watching the Company at practice that evening, Grace was surprised by what looked like the confusion of a real battle, almost as though Dizzy was right and there had been a press photographer present in 1360. What she was looking at reminded her of riots, people grappling hand-to-hand with police. Never mind artillery, air cover, nuclear missiles — this was how people had always fought, would always fight, if they could get at each other. The biggest picture was a long shot of the battlefield, while in the foreground an archer was loosing an arrow above them. The shot had been taken from very low down, almost from between the archer's knees.

'Dangerous,' Dad said, pointing to the arrow. 'What happens to the audience?'

'How big's your arena?' Gareth said. 'Not many longbowmen can exceed three hundred yards; our crew would be lucky to hit two hundred. We don't shoot into the crowd, and anyway, they use birding blunts. And for safety there has to be eighteen inches of fletching on the arrows.'

'Just a minute,' Dad said. Grace saw that he was getting interested in spite of himself. 'Fletching's the feathers, isn't it? *Eighteen inches?*'

'Equal to eighteen inches, say six flights of three inches each. Maximizes the aerodynamic drag. Slows it down.'

'And what's your birding blunt when it's at home?'

'You wouldn't go wild-fowling with a war arrow,' Gareth said, reasonably. 'You take your bird out with a blunt bolt, literally knock it off.'

'You go wild-fowling with one of *those*?'

'I don't go wild-fowling at all, I'm a vegetarian,' Gareth said. 'Anyway, we needn't have our bowmen along unless you want them. What we'd stage is a combat between infantry –'

'What about Hendrickje?' Dizzy said. Grace elbowed her into silence.

'And maybe a couple of mounted men on the fringes. It improves the look of the thing; people like to see horses. We could probably do it on our own but if you want I could call up another society to swell the numbers.'

'You list yourselves in *Yellow Pages*?' Dad said. 'What under?'

Gareth brought out a magazine from his file. 'This is the re-enactment Yellow Pages,' he said. '*Call to Arms*. Everyone's in here. Even us.'

'What do you mean, *even* you?' Dad looked suspicious, as if he were being sold a pup.

'White Horse is a relatively new society, a splinter group from Sir Aylmer's Mercenaries and the remains of a disbanded Dark Age outfit who've gained four centuries overnight. Strictly speaking we're soldiers of fortune, a Free Company.'

'Light's dawning,' Dad said. He turned to Grace. 'Weren't you asking me about all this a week or two back?'

Grace remembered. The telescope! 'It must have been when I first met Dizzy,' she mumbled.

'Now, how free are you?' Dad said. 'Are you just going to turn up and knock hell out of each other, or do we get a proper show?'

'All we need is a script,' Gareth said, 'which we can turn out half an hour before we start. It won't be a free-for-all, but it won't be choreographed either. You'll see real fighting.'

Dad sat silently for a moment, then he said, 'Right, you're on. Clear out, girls. We're going to talk booking fees. This is business.'

Grace, not wanting to be reminded of booking fees, beckoned Dizzy out into the garden and was just closing the door behind her when Dad called her back.

'Auntie!'

'Yes, Dad?'

'You done good, girl. You're forgiven.'

Dizzy, Grace and Frank sat in a row in the cab of the Fordson. Grace, in the middle, crouched between the bucket seats.

'So,' Frank said, arms folded on the steering wheel, 'Gareth and the gang are fighting at the rally.'

'Are you going to join the White Horse?' Grace said. 'Salvo is.'

'Oh, *do*,' Dizzy begged him, 'then we'll all be in it.'

Frank looked pleased. 'Yer, all right,' he said. 'If they'll have me.'

'If you're going to be an armourer you'll have to be in it.'

It hadn't struck Grace before that Frank might feel sad and unwanted too. He didn't even have a girlfriend at present, and there was Salvo with two to choose from. Frank would never be envious of Salvo, he admired him too much, but he could be moody and sullen. She looked at him smiling at Dizzy, who only liked Frank because she liked everybody, and she thought how seldom it was that she saw Frank smile.

His head cocked sideways as though he were pricking an ear, like a dog hearing a can being opened. 'BMW,' said Frank. 'Yours?'

'Oh, it's Daddy.' Dizzy fumbled to open the door handle. Halfway out, balancing with one foot on the step, she stopped. 'Or Mummy.' And swarmed back inside.

'Ha,' Frank said. He craned his neck to see out

of the cab's small rear window, into the street. 'Mummy *and* Daddy,' he announced. 'Fear not, man, Sir Frank will save you. Get your head down, Diz.'

Wiping his hands on the seat of his jeans and looking studiedly gormless, Frank slouched down the path.

'Hi, Bill,' he said. 'Evening, Mrs M.'

'O-o-oh,' Dizzy moaned, from under the dashboard. 'She *hates* people talking to her like that.'

Good, Grace thought savagely.

'Is Dizzy here?' they heard Mrs Morley asking. 'We rang the farm and Marian seemed to think she might be.'

'Yer, sure,' Frank said. 'Come on in, man.' Mummy was no doubt expecting the front door but Frank led them past the Fordson and through the side gate, tapping reassuringly on the side of the cab as he went by. Clever Frank, handing Mummy over to Dad and Gareth before she got anywhere near Dizzy. A few minutes later he came back. 'Go in now,' he said. 'Don't want to miss the fun.'

They climbed down from the cab and followed him indoors just as another car pulled up behind the BMW. Grace, seeing that it was their own Vauxhall, hung back. Out got Salvo and Birgitta.

'Hey, man,' Salvo mouthed. 'Wait-wait. What going on, man? Marian rang the pub and said Mummy was on the warpath. Reinforcements is here, man.'

They all entered the kitchen together. There were rarely more than four people around the table, now there were nine: Bill Morley and Gareth, Dad, Frank, Salvo, Birgitta, Grace and Dizzy. Squeezed into the corner by the door was Mummy, squeezed not only by the weight of numbers but by Bill and Gareth, who were clasping each other by the elbows like old comrades who had not met for ten years.

'I knew it!' Gareth was yelling. 'I knew you'd come back. It's the old sword itch. Arise and put your armour on.'

'Bring me my bow of burning gold, *yeah*,' Salvo said. 'Likewise my arrows of desire. Bill, man, you joining the White Horse too?'

'In his heart he never went away,' Gareth said.

'Used to be with Sir Aylmer's . . . pressures of work . . . away in the Gulf . . . difficult . . .' Bill Morley mumbled. He did not look at his wife.

'The sword itch never leaves you,' Gareth said. 'Like the war horse that smelleth the battle afar off and saith ha, ha, among the trumpets.'

There was silence, as they all waited for Mummy to say something. Grace, feeling Dizzy tremble at her side, knew that if Mrs Morley could have turned them all to stone, starting with Gareth and Salvo, she would have done it. At last she forced a brave smile and said the nicest thing she could think of.

'It looks as if the lunatics have taken over the asylum.'

Dad gave her a mad little bow. 'You're so right, ma'am. One touch of lunacy makes the whole world kin.'

Chapter Twelve

The programmes had arrived. They stood in blocks on the living-room table, like a set of giant Lego bricks, with the cardboard carton that contained the brass commemorative plaques. Grace took a programme and leafed through it, searching among the entries for the ones that mattered. *No. 415: 1930 Lister A 3 hp driving cattle cake mill. Owners Mr R. and Mrs J. Thompson.* That was the stationary engine. *No. 583: 1947 Fordson Thames 7V 4ton Dropside Lorry. Owner C. Salvatore.* It was there in the programme, in black and white. Unfortunately, that was as far as it was going.

'Do you mean to tell me,' Dad had said, 'that it's *not* going to be ready after all?'

After Grace had found the wheeling machine, after Salvo had made the mudguards, after all that they had forgotten to tax and insure it. Once Gareth had turned them loose on the contents of John James St Leger's armoury, the Fordson had been relegated to the second division.

'Anyway,' Salvo said, 'if we tried to get it completely finished it would be a rush job. I'm never going to get the edges of those skirts turned in time. It wouldn't be right. Never mind, Ron, you *know* it'll be ready for next year.'

'I don't know any such thing,' Dad said. 'You'll have found something else to play with by then.'

That had been on Saturday. On Sunday they coaxed Mum and Dad up to Gareth and Marian's to have a look at the Company in action.

'I suppose we have to consult you too, these days,' Dad said to Grace. 'Are you coming with us?'

'Yes, please. I'll come back with Dizzy and her dad,' Grace said.

'Are you sure they don't mind you being round there all the time?' Mum asked.

'I shouldn't think they'd notice,' Dad said. 'I shouldn't think they'd notice if she moved in. The place is the size of an hotel.' He had been up there already with Bill and seen for himself.

'Frank and Salvo *have* moved in,' Grace said. They had taken sleeping bags and installed themselves in the room above the workshop, so as to spend all their spare time on the wheeling machine, making a coat of plates for Gareth. At night they amused themselves on the stairs, recreating the Shadow, in the hope that some foolhardy person out late on the footpath would see it and be frightened into fits.

'And what does Mrs Morley have to say to all this?' Mum wanted to know, as they drove to Sternham.

'She hasn't *said* anything.' Grace had not even seen Mummy since the memorable Wednesday night when she had appeared in the Thompsons' kitchen. Mum had never seen her at all, but she had heard plenty.

'She is going to Wales,' Birgitta had reported, meaning that she had already gone. 'She is going to see a – a –' she searched for the right word, '– a dead person, in the ground.'

'A funeral?'

'Ah, yes. A funeral.'

'It was a wedding last week.'

'She knows a lot of people,' Dizzy said.

When they arrived at the farm the house was empty, so Grace took them straight through the garden gate to watch the combat in the meadow. She had said nothing to Mum and Dad about shanty town; she wanted it to be a surprise.

It had rained on Saturday night and the mud of the yard was as soft as melting chocolate. 'There's a sort of hard path through the middle,' Grace said, going ahead, 'where Marian puts the cinders. You won't sink in.' She found that she was talking to air. Mum and Dad were still standing in the gateway, staring at the derelicts and junk that surrounded them.

When the shock wore off they advanced, dazedly, and began poking about under sacking and plastic.

'Do they know what they've got here?' Mum said. She had discovered the boiler of the stationary engine.

'That tractor,' Dad said. 'It's a Marshall 15/30. I'll swear it's a 15/30.'

Marian was coming towards them from the meadow, skirts gathered up in one hand, sloshing along the cinder track in Wellington boots. Grace was about to introduce them, but Dad had no time for formalities.

'This is all yours? Are you doing anything with it?'

'Doing anything?' Marian said. 'It was all here when we came. One day I expect we'll get around to shifting it. The last owners went bankrupt and the land was sold separately, but we got the house and two acres at auction. All this came with it.'

'That's how Dizzy got the wheeling machine,' Grace said.

'Yes, but the wheeling machine was in good condition, mainly because they kept it in the kitchen. I'm not surprised they went bankrupt.' Marian flapped a defeated hand at the yard. 'When we can afford to we'll get someone to clear it out.'

'Get someone to clear it out?' Dad looked scandalized. 'Don't you want it?'

'No,' Marian said. 'I don't want it. I don't want any of it.' She saw the look in their eyes.

'Are you trying to tell me you *do* want it? You'd actually take it *away?*'

'Not all at once,' Mum said cautiously, before Dad could begin to make rash arrangements about the low-loader. 'But there's some valuable stuff here. If you got photos taken we could display them at Arling. There'd be a lot of interest.'

Grace left them to it. Not thirty metres away the Company of the White Horse was engaged in mortal combat, but Mum and Dad had not even noticed. They had eyes only for the horsebox, the tractor, the potato riddler and the stationary engine. Mum was saying, 'Ron, *Ron*, it's an Armstrong-Whitworth!'

'You think you've got room for a coal lorry here?' Dad said.

'I thought you were talking about *removing* –'

'Hang about. Could you fit the Fordson in somewhere? Out the front, maybe?'

'Oh, the Fordson. I've heard about the Fordson.'

'Haven't we all,' Dad said. 'And it still won't be ready on time. No what I was thinking, Mrs – Miss – Marian, if we got the Fordson out of our drive, we'd have room for some of this stuff, say the engine and the Marshall.'

Perhaps Mummy was right, Grace thought, going to sit in the hedge till the Company had finished. Perhaps they were lunatics, Mum and Dad, Salvo and Frank and Gareth, and Dizzy's dad, and Marian with her candles and crystals. But even if they were sad, like Frank, or fed up, like Marian, or hard up, like the Thompsons, they

177

had their own ways of dealing with it. No one else suffered and in a sense they understood each other. They were all mad about something. It was *being* mad that mattered.

With his bascinet on, Grace had not recognized Bill Morley among the fray, until he came off the field with Gareth.

'Dizzy with you?' he said.

'Salvo's borrowed a jeep. He's bringing her with the others for the council of war.'

'We don't actually need them for the council of war,' Gareth said. 'None of them is fighting. Where did he get hold of a jeep? What year is it?'

'We had an idea,' Grace said, 'for how we could be in it.'

'You can't be in it,' Gareth said. 'No non-combatants on the field during battle. It's a rule we have to observe, no exceptions.'

'What about before you start?'

'What *is* all this?' Gareth said. 'You're plotting. Come clean.'

'Not plotting,' Grace said. 'Not going behind your back. But we had an idea how we could all be in it, all of us. Even the goats.'

'The goats?' Bill Morley said. 'Do I detect the hand of Salvo in all this?'

'Just a bit,' Grace said, 'but it was me as well, after Marian said that sometimes she went to battles with you. I told Salvo and he said it was a shame to waste so much talent.'

'Are you sure he meant the goats and not Birgitta?' Gareth said.

*

Marian danced in the doorway, twirling her orange scarf and singing, 'It's started. It's started. It's begun.' She had just seen off Mum and Dad and four cast-iron fly wheels.

'What's begun?' Gareth said, from his seat at the head of the table.

'Nothing, darling.' Marian paused, kissed the top of his head, and danced away again. 'Just moving a few things. In six months' time,' she said to the others, 'when everything has gone, he'll walk in one morning and say, "Is something missing?"'

She sat down at the opposite end of the table. 'Everyone here?' Gareth said. They were all there: Salvo, Birgitta and Frank on one side, Dizzy and her father next to Grace. All my friends, Grace thought, looking up and down the table.

'Right,' Gareth said, nodding at Salvo. 'Fire away.'

'OK, man. Now, I'm not interfering in your combat, man, but you said you needed a script. How much script? Written down?'

'Nothing like that,' Gareth said. 'All we need is an excuse to fight and a plan of action. We don't just wade in and lay on. Remember, we're mercenaries, looking for someone to pay our wages. We've been fighting the French for as long as we can remember; now King Edward's signed a treaty and we're at a loose end. We aren't interested in kings and treaties. As far as we're concerned, we're going to go on fighting the French. That is what we do.'

'You ever been to a rally, man?' Frank said.

'No.'

'Well, what'll happen is that all that'll get read out over the PA system. Arling's a big place. And,' he tried to be tactful, 'it doesn't sound all that interesting, especially if people don't know who you are.'

'What we thought, man,' Salvo interposed, hurriedly, 'is that if you were going to mauraud a village, we could maybe lay on the village.'

'I don't think we're up to anything that elaborate,' Gareth said.

'Not elaborate, man; *people*,' Salvo said. 'People and livestock.'

'The goats,' Bill murmured.

'And the donkey, and the girls – ladies –'

'Women, Salvo,' Marian suggested.

'– the female element, could be peaceful peasants, tending flocks and similar, and then someone can rush in yelling, "Here come mad Sir Gareth and his Merry Men!" Panic, screams, stampede of goats etcetera; out rush the menfolk to defend the womenfolk and the battle commences. Meanwhile all non-combatants is cowering in the bushes; that'd be the Invicta Pavilion, probably. Let's face it, man,' Salvo said, 'you got Birgitta and Marian just strolling about, you won't need no PA system. Everyone will stop to watch.'

Grace was afraid that Gareth was going to turn it down flat. Worse, Marian might turn it down flat. They were, after all, her goats and her donkey, and she did not seem to be all that keen on re-enactment anyway. But it was Marian who spoke first.

'Considering Salvo's never done anything like this before, it sounds like a good idea,' she said. 'But you'll need more men. Have you heard from Sir Aylmer yet?'

'He's letting us have nine foot soldiers. We'll do without bowmen.'

'Weren't they the lot you split up from?' Frank said. 'Will it be safe to have them on the battlefield?'

'All water under the bridge,' Bill said. 'We shan't be settling old scores, if that's what you're afraid of.'

Gareth picked up his copy of *Call to Arms* and tapped the cover. 'See what it says here? *Never in Anger*. That's the watchword. No one does this to cause harm. If you want to see real dirty fighting, go to a football match.'

'You mean we can be in it?' Dizzy said. She turned to her father. 'Can *I*?' Grace could guess the unspoken question, *What will Mummy say*?

'I think we can work it out,' Bill said. 'Now Frank, Grace, you're the experts. What happens between now and Saturday?'

'Nothing happens till Thursday,' Frank said, 'and then everything happens.'

Mum had a friend with a word processor, and came home with thousands of slips printed in Gothic letters: *3 p.m. Medieval Combat with The Company of the White Horse and Sir Aylmer's Mercenaries*, in three different sizes. Salvo took the largest and pasted them on to the posters that were already erected. The smaller ones were stuck to fliers which

Frank, on roller skates, distributed as dusk fell, stapling them to telephone poles and fence posts. The smallest ones had to be slipped into the programmes, four thousand of them.

'Ought to make you stick *them* in,' Dad said severely to Grace. She and Dizzy and Helen formed a kind of production line at the living room table, Dizzy opening the programmes and Helen running a felt tip through *Thrills and Spills with the Motomaniax Stunt Team*. Grace, on the end, put in the correction slips and closed the programme. That took care of Tuesday and Wednesday.

'I don't know why I'm doing this,' Helen grumbled. 'It's nothing to do with me.' She said this every year; every year she refused to have anything to do with the rally until the last moment, and then got as involved as the rest of them.

'Do you want to be in the re-enactment with us?' asked Dizzy, who would have invited everyone to join in, given the chance.

'No thanks, but I'll watch,' Helen said. 'Now that Frank's found his true station in life, I want to be there to see.'

'What's that?'

'A peasant,' Helen said.

Marian turned up on Wednesday morning, driving the Austin-Healey, with Birgitta and a bundle of clothes for the poor peasants, which she draped over Grace and Dizzy. 'If they don't fit, gird them up with rope,' she said to Dizzy, who looked like a statue waiting to be unveiled. 'This is war-torn Burgundy, remember. A smart turn-out was the last thing on people's minds. That lot in the bag's for Frank.'

'What about shoes?'

'Barefoot. Just watch out for thistles.'

'Suppose it rains?'

'We get wet. The umbrella was not invented till the eighteenth century. Anyway, we're only going to be on show for a few minutes.'

'Don't we come back afterwards?'

'No, we'll all be dead, but for safety reasons we have to die off-stage. The goats of course will be eaten. Which reminds me, Birgitta, don't let me forget to ring the cat-sitter. Now, Gareth wants to know when he can go up and look at the arena.'

'There isn't any arena yet,' Grace said. 'Just grass. We all go up there tomorrow and get things ready.'

'You do?'

'Dad and the committee,' Helen said. 'The rest of us go along as gofers. If Gareth shows up around five everything will be marked out by ropes; the arena and the sites for the different classes. It has to be done by then because the traction engines start arriving. And there's the funfair to set up – well, you'll see.'

'I'll tell him, and I'll collect you girls this evening for a practice. You'd better get Frank along. The Company don't need to be there, but we've got to work out our moves and timing; we must be clear of the arena before one armed man sets foot in it. Right, have I forgotten anything?'

'Salvo,' Birgitta said.

'Salvo declines to be a peasant,' Marian said.

'He says he's stewarding, which is a lousy excuse, I think.'

'Oh no,' Grace said. 'He's on standby for the stationary engines in case Rachel has her baby during the rally.'

'I'm sure you're right,' Marian said, 'but I don't quite follow.'

'Our sister-in-law,' Helen said. 'Due on Saturday. Mum'll be looking after her kids if she's on time, which means that Salvo will have to take over, not that he knows the first thing about stationary engines.'

'And he helps Dad with the vehicle movements,' Grace said. 'You know, when they're moving from their stands to the arena.'

'That's one of my favourite sights,' Helen said. 'Salvo, standing in front of a steamroller. My very favourite is Salvo and Frank standing in front of a steamroller.' She caught Birgitta's angry eye. 'All I meant,' she explained, 'was that if Salvo was *flat* you could stick him in a book like a pressed flower and keep him for ever.'

Fifty years ago and more, Spitfires and Hurricanes had flown from Arling airfield to fight the Battle of Britain. Dad could remember it. As a boy he had watched them take off, and counted them back in.

All that was left of those glory days were three asphalt roads and a couple of buildings that had been rescued from collapse and were now called pavilions. Invicta Pavilion had once been the Officers' Mess, and if you knew where to find it there was still a painting on a wall of a lady who looked, Grace knew now, just like Georgiana Ledbetter without any clothes on.

The rest of the airfield was grass. Now, with the sun setting, long shadows lay across it; solid tree shadows and the spindly, spidery shadows of hundreds of iron stakes linked by rope and plastic tape that had turned the airfield into a ghost town, with skeleton streets and skeleton car parks. At every corner signs had been erected: TO THE FUNFAIR, TO THE VETERAN CARS, MILITARY VEHICLES, STATIONARY ENGINES, TOILETS, BAR, CAMP SITE THIS WAY.

And that was all. Apart from the Thompsons' Vauxhall, Salvo's borrowed jeep and the Big Healey, there was not a vehicle in sight. On the Thursday before a rally, Grace's family was always the first to turn up and the last to leave. Tomorrow the funfair would arrive and set up, along with the Mortier organ, which was as big as a bus, and the traction engines. Until this year Grace had always managed to talk Dad into letting her go up to Arling with him on the Friday to watch the steamers make their entrance, a whole day before the other exhibitors. From the main gate to the corner by the Portaloos stood a row of booths where the stewards sat throughout the rally. The Thompsons' booth was on the end, nearest to the gate, and there Grace would sit for the whole day, under strict instructions not to move, watching the fair arrive and the great glossy smoking engines trundle past on the way to their enclosure.

This year, however, Grace would have other things to attend to on Friday. She felt almost sorry about that, almost nostalgic, as she walked the grass streets with Dizzy, killing time until Dad called them over to the car. Things would never be quite the same again. They might be better, but they would not be the same.

They paused at a junction where their grass road crossed asphalt.

'This'll be the funfair on that bit, between here and the trees,' Grace said. 'Traction engines are opposite and the military vehicles over there. And auto jumble's just here.'

Dizzy looked all around. The evening wind was shivering the long grass under the trees and the air was turning cool.

'Supposing nobody comes? Suppose it rains?'

'Thousands of people will come,' Grace said. 'Even if it does rain. There were over fourteen thousand here last year. It isn't going to rain – the weather forecast said so. It won't rain till next week. Anyway, didn't you get on to the Blessed Damozel?'

'Of course I did. And we can both work on her tomorrow night.'

Grace was spending Friday night at 19 Rectory Lane, where there were four spare bedrooms. Dizzy was coming home to the Close with her tonight as, with Frank dossing down over the workshop, there was actually a spare room at home, and Helen, surprisingly, had volunteered to move in there so that Grace and Dizzy could share.

That was the sort of thing that was starting to happen, Grace thought; it was as if she had suddenly turned into a person, part of the household, someone who had to be taken into account. She had secretly been hoping that it might happen on her eleventh birthday, with a kind of fanfare, as the family finally welcomed her as one of themselves, but the birthday was still three weeks away and yet everything had changed already, without anyone being aware of it. She had hardly been aware of it herself.

Over towards the gate, by the line of booths, someone was calling.

'Come on,' Grace said, ducking under the nearest tape. 'We'll take a short cut.' They ran across the enclosure where already stalls were set up for the auto jumble; along the edge of the Mortier organ stand and past the place where the beer tent would be pitched, hitting the road again opposite the Portaloos.

'Do you know it all by heart?' Dizzy said, as they slowed down to walk the last bit.

'A lot of it stays the same,' Grace said. 'It depends how many exhibits there are in each class. If we got a lot of extra fire engines or something, we'd have to make the commercial vehicle enclosure bigger, and that would mean somewhere else being smaller, but there's always plenty of room. Most of it's just like last year, except for the birds of prey.'

'Hawks?' Dizzy said. 'Will there be hawks? They flew hawks in the Middle Ages. Do they fly them here? I wonder if Gareth –'

'A lot of them are owls,' Grace said. 'They're from a sanctuary. They aren't very exciting, Diz. Mostly they just sit there with their heads going round, glaring at people. But they can't come this year. Doesn't matter, though. They go in that big space in the middle of the auto jumble. It'll just stay empty.'

'No, it won't,' Dad said, as they came up to him. 'That's where you'll be.'

'Me?'

'The battle,' Dad said. 'The main arena's far too big.'

'We could stage a tournament in the main arena,' Gareth said thoughtfully. He was sitting in the Transport steward's booth.

'We could, but we shan't,' Marian said decidedly. 'No, if the Company fights in the main arena the spectators will be so far away they won't know what's happening. They'll probably think it's hooligans scrapping and someone will call the rozzers. That enclosure for the birds of prey is perfect. Everyone will get a good view.'

'Auto jumble's popular,' Dad said. 'There'll be a lot of people around.'

'And it's near the beer tent,' Gareth said.

Later, as they lay in bed, Grace said, 'Is your mum back from Wales yet?' She was wondering about tomorrow night, and what kind of a reception she would get at Rectory Lane.

'Oh, yes,' Dizzy said. 'She came back on Tuesday, I think.'

'She doesn't mind me stopping?'

There was a long silence. Then Dizzy said, 'We *are* friends, aren't we? Proper friends. Just us. Doesn't-matter-what-anyone-else-thinks.'

'Of course we are,' Grace said, half expecting what was coming next.

There was another silence, then Dizzy said, 'Yes, she does mind, and she minds me coming here. She wouldn't have let me, only Daddy had already said yes. I don't know what'll happen when Daddy goes back to Abu Dhabi. And she'll give Birgitta the sack. I know she will.'

'Why? What's she done?'

'Because of Salvo,' Dizzy said. 'I'll come home one Friday and she won't be there. That's what always happens. There was Eva, before that. She was nice, but she just went. Mummy made her go and she never said why.'

Grace could hear her trying not to cry. 'I don't think that will happen to Birgitta,' she said. 'She could go to Marian and Gareth or something. They're friends, aren't they? It'll be all right.'

Dizzy sniffed, unconvinced. 'Do you think so?'

'Yes, I do. Things will get easier,' Grace said, and as she said it, she was sure of it. 'They *will*, Diz. It's getting easier already. Haven't you noticed how much people notice *us*? You and me?'

'Do they?' Dizzy said. Grace saw her sit up in the darkness. 'But we don't do anything.'

'No,' Grace agreed, 'we don't. But we make things happen.'

Chapter Thirteen

Grace stood at the end of the main arena
and gazed down the length of it, a long
acre of grass, churned and flattened round
the edge in an oval, where the motorbikes, the
commercial vehicles, the veteran and classic cars
had already made their parades for the day. Now
the tractors were grinding their way round. The
final parades would be the historic transport, the
military vehicles and last of all, as the climax,
the traction engines.

Grace hardly saw the tractors. All she could
think of were those hundreds of faces watching
them, hundreds of faces that might shortly be

watching her. Suppose they were disappointed? Suppose they booed and demanded their money back because they were not seeing the promised motorcycle stunts? Suppose they refused to leave the main arena to watch the battle and stayed sullenly here, staring at nothing, waiting for the buses? But they would never do that. It was a huge and happy crowd, gathered in sunshine on a summer Saturday, determined to have a good time.

Everyone was here who mattered. She had seen all her friends from school in the crowd, the Milners, Steffi and Sarah, the Claggetts, even the Charters from next door, in a good mood for once. Everyone was here except Mum. Mum was at Gavin's, glued to the phone for a message from the hospital where Rachel was having her baby, ready to pass it on to Dad, who had borrowed a mobile phone for the occasion.

The tractors had stopped circling and were beginning to leave the arena at the far end. The commentator, who was out in the middle with a microphone, where he had been interviewing the tractor drivers, called the crowd to attention.

'Ladies and Gentlemen! As you know, we were to have been entertained this afternoon by the Motomaniax stunt team and, as you know, this cannot now take place. They have been prevented from attending by a serious accident, but, happily, no fatalities and we wish them a speedy recovery!'

The crowd made a moaning sound of sympathy.

'But, Ladies and Gentlemen, to make up for

that we have a spectacle no less thrilling: the first appearance in public of the Company of the White Horse, supported by Sir Aylmer's Mercenaries, who will re-enact a medieval combat. As no vehicles are involved, ha ha, this will take place in the lower arena, next to the auto jumble, in fifteen minutes. We have adjusted the schedule to give you time to make your way there. It's only a hundred yards or so, Ladies and Gentlemen, so if you would like to start moving towards the lower arena . . .'

Grace wished that he had not mentioned the auto jumble. It made things sound so crusty, even though the arena was properly staked out. She was lingering to make sure that the crowd really did begin to move when a voice said, 'Get your skates on, Auntie,' and a sleeve in a steward's red armband nudged her shoulder. Salvo had come up behind her. 'Go and get changed. Dizzy's already on her way. Don't waste a minute.'

Grace began running up the field towards the row of stewards' booths, where she could see Marian waving frantically. Mum and Dad always pitched a tent next to their booth, where Mum kept a kettle going on a camping stove and where they could retreat if the weather turned nasty. Today the peasants were using it as a dressing room. The Company were making do with a canvas screen behind Sir Aylmer's minibus.

Grace wasted the forbidden minute by looking in at the booth where Dad was sitting alone, dealing with enquiries. Any moment now she might become an aunt for the sixth time, but she would not know about it till afterwards.

'Come *on*,' Dizzy cried, hopping about in agitation in the doorway of the tent. 'We're all ready. We thought you'd forgotten.'

Grace scrambled into her costume and took the band off her hair so that it hung loose down her back. Dizzy's hair was short and wavy, not at all medieval, so she was wearing a hood and pretending to be a boy. There was another reason for this, as Grace discovered when she came out of the tent to find the rest of the peasants waiting for her, and they all moved off towards the arena.

Birgitta led the way with the three goats on rope leads. Like Marian she had plaited her long hair into two braids that hung down on either side of her face, almost hiding her ears but not quite concealing the fact that in the right one she was wearing a perfect amber teardrop, the colour of marmalade. Marian, beside her, carried a pole with a clump of fleece at one end, like candy floss. She said it was her distaff and from the other hand her spindle hung on a length of spun yarn. Frank, who had bobbed his hair for a real peasant look and was dressed in sacking, led Jenny the donkey, heavily laden with bales across her back, although Grace knew they were bean bags and weighed almost nothing. Dizzy came last of all, leading Hendrickje with her right hand: the squire and the destrier.

At the end of the lower arena, behind a row of auto-jumble stalls, Sir Gareth and Sir Aylmer were walking along the lines of their companies, checking sword blades to make sure that they were of regulation thickness. When they were satisfied, Sir Aylmer's men, who were to defend the village, climbed into the minibus and drove round to the far end of the arena, so as not to be seen by the gathering crowd. Gareth, his helm under his arm, walked over to Dizzy and claimed Hendrickje.

A voice, horribly distorted by the PA system, began bawling.

'And now, Ladies and Gentlemen, young men and maidens, we are to see a display the like of which has never before graced this hallowed turf of Arling.'

'Jeez, he's worse than Gareth,' Marian said. 'Where do they find these people?'

'That's Salvo,' Grace said.

'Whoops!' said Marian.

'Before your very eyes history will live again, as Sir Aylmer's Mercenaries and the Company of the White Horse fight to the death for your delectation. Ladies and Gentlemen, etcetera, I implore you. We are about to begin. Don't hang about, get your sweet selves over here but *now*!'

'I didn't think he'd be able to keep that up,' Marian said. 'Now, all remember what you're doing? Good luck! We're on.'

The crowd around the arena was loud with excitement. The Mortier organ was playing Sousa marches at full volume, one of the fairground rides was belting out *Pineapple Rag*, all around engines were revving, the steamer whistles were shrilling in the distance, and 30,000 feet up a Boeing 747 was heading for Europe. But the arena was silent; the silence of a time before aircraft, organs, engines. It was 1360, and the only sound was a skylark. Grace, hearing it, looked up and saw it.

'Ladies and Gentlemen,' Salvo announced, 'the time, the Middle Ages. The place, a meadow in France. A band of English mercenaries is approaching . . .'

It was Frank who went first, with Jenny, greeted by friendly hoots and whistles in the crowd from mates who recognized him, but they too were quiet when Birgitta followed him, leading the goats, and then Marian, spinning as she walked. The crowd sighed happily and looked towards the entrance in the hope of seeing more pretty girls, but it was Dizzy who came next, turning cartwheels and handsprings. I didn't know she could do that, Grace thought vaguely.

She waited, with clenched fists, as the peasants spread out over the arena, only now it was a meadow, peaceful, sunlit. The lark sang on. 'Count to ninety after Dizzy goes in,' Marian had told her. 'Count slowly; say "and" between each number. That will give us one and a half minutes.'

'Seventy and seventy-one and seventy-two and . . .' Frank was two-thirds of the way across. 'Eighty-four and eighty-five and eighty-six . . .' Now Dizzy had reached the middle. 'Eighty-nine and *ninety*.' She looked behind her to get the signal from Gareth. He was not there.

Looking down at her was a great black warhorse, and on its back, outlined against the blue sky, a towering figure in mail and habergeon, with shining armour plates on its limbs, a lance in its mailed fist. There was no face. The great helm with its slit, expressionless eyes, stared down where she cowered, miles below. It was not Gareth who sat there on Hendrickje, nice Gareth on his elderly mare; it was an armed and expert killer, without pity, without mercy, who would ride her down on his destrier and ride on, to kill again. The figure raised its lance. She turned and ran screaming into the arena.

'The English are coming! The English are coming!'

They all turned as she hurtled towards them, and took up the cry: 'The English are coming!' Frank slapped Jenny across the quarters and they cantered out of the arena together, Birgitta fled with the goats, tangled and stumbling. Dizzy shrieked, ran to Grace and fell, bringing them both down. Marian ran back, dragged them to their feet, and together the three of them raced for safety. As they reached the far exit Grace heard a roar from the crowd and looked round to see Gareth cantering into the arena, followed by the Company.

The village peasants, in their pitiful scraps of armour, ran out in the opposite direction and they all met in the middle while Gareth and Hendrickje circled them until a retainer ran up and took Hendrickje's bridle to lead her away while Gareth dismounted, sword drawn, and charged on foot into the fray.

'A good panic, though I say it myself. I think

we'll keep it in the act,' Marian said. Only then did Grace remember that it was an act. She did not think that even when she saw the shadow on the whitewashed window she had been as terrified as when she saw Gareth waiting to charge and understood for the first time what a knight really looked like, what a knight really was.

Still shaking a little she stood with the others to watch the fight, as the surging mass of warriors broke up and became skirmishes at strategic points around the perimeter, where everyone would get a good view. People were shouting and applauding, the crowd was growing by the minute as more came to watch. And a voice near by was saying, 'Why do they call themselves the White Horse, Betty? That's what I want to know. That was a black horse, wasn't it, Betty? Wasn't that a black horse he was riding? Wasn't it? Why do they want to call themselves a white horse?'

'White Horse of Kent, madam,' a voice shouted behind them. 'Invicta!' Grace looked round and saw Salvo beside her, one arm round Birgitta, the other hand wielding the microphone. Birgitta was still leading the goats.

'There's always one,' Salvo said, nodding at the white horse lady. 'Now, do you want the good news or the bad news, Auntie?'

'The bad news.' He was grinning. It couldn't be that bad, then.

'Just been hearing the latest weather forecast. They changed their tiny minds. Heavy rain all day tomorrow over the South-east.'

Grace grinned back. It didn't matter if an

earthquake swallowed Arling airfield tomorrow. They were having their moment of glory now. 'What's the good news?'

'Message from your mum, just in. You've got another niece, Auntie.'

'Oh.' Nieces, who needed them? 'Is it all right?'

'She, not it. Naomi Rose Thompson. Eight pounds and an ounce. Mother and baby doing well. Hear that, Dizzy? Auntie's an aunt again.'

In the arena Sir Aylmer and Sir Gareth had hewn their way towards each other and were about to engage in single combat. The crowd shouted, starting to take sides and rooting for one or the other.

'Go for it, Gareth,' the peasants yelled, although it was their village that he was about to demolish. Salvo took advantage of his microphone to drown out the opposition.

'GO FOR IT, GARETH!' He put his spare arm round Grace and Dizzy. 'Hey, man,' Salvo said. 'This is Cloud Nine. This is Nirvana, man. I haven't had so much fun since the pipes burst at the cop shop.'